DARK YONDER

ISSUE 9

APRIL 2025

CONTENTS

FROM THE EDITORS

Dear Dark Yonderers,

I hope you enjoy the new look of our book. It's our third year and ninth volume and we're starting 2025 with a sharp left hook. One of my favorite moments in putting together this book was receiving the submission email from Ms Vicki Hendricks, who mentioned her credits, which I thought was beautiful considering the author of *Miami Purity* would ever have to introduce herself to the likes of me. Consider me a HUGE fan. We're also pleased as punch to bring Gary Phillips to the *Dark Yonder* fold with his banging little tale, "Biff-Bam the Magic Man."

Want some repeat offenders? I love picking up a Mike McHone story wherever I can find one and the master is back on our pages again with "Domestic." And fans of the *BAMS 2023* author Fleur Bradley will love to hear that she's picked up that little blue book again in "How To Psycho-Analyze Yourself."

"Blood is Blood," writes Sean Jacques and you'll want to wear a raincoat to make sure you don't get any on you. So happy to have CW Blackwell published here and you will be too because his "The Golden Age Fallacy" will bring a twisted little smile to your face.

Susan R. Morritt will make sure you never look at a bog quite the same way again with "Hello, Marylou." Winner of the Best Title Award goes to Jon Horn's little ditty, "Benny the Booster and Chlamydia Jane," while Robert Slentz-Kesler sprinkles a little cringe with "The Wishes of the Bishop."

But if there's one I'm most excited to bring to y'all this edition, it's "Comment Section," by Jim Ruland. It's an ambitious attempt and I think he pulls it off. A story told completely from the creepiest, most disgusting place in our world's history: the internet's comment section.

Special thanks to my co-editor, Katy Munger, for pulling all these together.

Y'all, let's enjoy the dark stuff.

—Eryk Pruitt

What Eryk said! Except to add, that as a lapsed Catholic — who still can't wrap her head around the fact that it is 2025, yet women can't be priests — I would like to point out that Robert Slentz-Kesler's "The Wishes of the Bishop" is cringe in a *good* way. It's also slightly insane, wonderfully chaotic, and surprisingly tasteful given the subject matter. You just can't teach that combo in a creative writing class. You either have it or you don't. And you will only find out if you have "it" in yourself if you take chances and let loose when you are writing. You know that stupid phrase written on Cracker Barrel-sold tea towels everywhere: "Dance like nobody's watching?" Well, if you want to find your voice and stand out, you have to write like nobody's reading. Only then you actually do have to go out and find people to read it to see if it works because, well, because when you're a writer... nothing is easy. Absolutely nothing. Which is why it's a good thing there's also nothing like the feeling of surfing on the edge of time itself when you get into the groove on a project you are working on and you are channeling something unique within you that wants to come out. Time stands still, yet evaporates at the same time. You lose yourself in the flow. There's no better feeling in the world, except maybe knowing that your writing touched other people, or moved them, or made them think outside their worlds when you were done.

All of this (yes, you guessed it) brings me to my particular editorial theme for Issue 9: every single one of the stories chosen for this issue has a very particular voice and a unique writing style, thanks to the courage of the author who wrote it. Of course, there are definitely more than a few surprises when it comes to plot twists and endings — but, for me, it's the writing itself that makes this issue. There are a few stories that use such an economical writing style that they are a joy to read. The lack of excess adjectives is like a balm to my soul. (You think I'm kidding? Trust me, I'm not the only editor that feels this way.) Others have such a dry, yet still almost wholesome, view of mankind that I just want to stand up and salute the author for keeping their sense of humor despite the world we live in right now. Still others managed to sustain a sweetly melancholy tone that aches with loss and regret throughout an entire story. That's not easy, trust me. But most of all, none of the writers in Issue 9 are trying to imitate another writer. None of them fall into cliched descriptions or plots. All of them somehow manage as authors to be present in their stories without being obtrusive, to put a new spin on some old themes, and make even the most hardboiled among us feel unexpectedly moved at times. I'm so impressed by them that my new life goal is to throw a party where every one of these writers in Issue 9 is present just to see what happens. Maybe we could do that at Yonder Cocktails and Bar in Hillsborough, N.C. one day? If so, the drinks are on Eryk. Oops, I mean, the drinks are on me. And I intend to demand that we all toast the occasion with a Jim Parker Strut (this issue's signature cocktail, which sounds like it could power a jet). But for now, I will content myself by thanking every writer in this issue for making me believe again in the power of voice. In the immortal words of many a man in a classic noir movie after he gets slapped so hard that his head snaps back, "Thanks! I needed that."

—Katy Munger

JIM PARKER'S STRUT

CALL ME BY MY NAME....

Winter is over, y'all, but it ain't quite summer. Consider this drink the go-between, although the argument can be made that this little doozy is good year-round. Just like its namesake, Jim Parker. One drink and it will have you strutting like Mick Jagger and just about as invincible. Don't believe me? Try one for yourself.

INGREDIENTS

1.5 oz Rhum Barbancourt (the pride of Haiti)
.5 oz overproof rum (at Yonder, we use Plantation)
1.5 oz pineapple juice
.75 oz ginger simple syrup
3 dashes Peychaud's bitters

DIRECTIONS

Shake all ingredients in a shaker, double strain over fresh ice, then add a wedge of fresh orange and a pineapple frond.

Enjoy!

BIFF-BAM, THE MAGIC MAN

GARY PHILLIPS

"BIFF DID YOU EVER KILL ANYONE?"

"What? Why in the world would you ask me that, Emery?" The school bus driver braked quickly, the vehicle groaning as a car in front of them unexpectantly zoomed away from the curb. He shook his head. Just another day... only not.

"Did you?" the young man persisted as the bus resumed travel. He sat where he always did, right behind the driver.

"What's this about? Would they let me drive you guys around if I had?"

"It was in the game, Biff."

He had no idea what game the kid was talking about. He turned the corner, their school taking up this end of the block. In the rearview mirror he could see Emery Patterson adjust his heavy glasses as he considered the question. "I guess not," the young man finally said. "But if you did kill someone, I bet they had it coming."

"Here we go. Time to get that learnin' on," he said, hoping to change the subject.

Bernard Steptoe, who the youngsters called Biff, guided

the type A bus across the blacktop to its designated spot on the roundabout. There were two long buses already in place as well. He shut off the engine and levered open the door. Out he stepped to operate the rear lift for the two youngsters in wheelchairs, Deb and Robin. When everyone was off-loaded, he walked back toward the door side of the bus. Emery was waiting for him with a grin on his face. His backpack was held by a strap in one hand, and with the other he leaned on his metal crutch.

"Seems to me you should write about your life, Biff. That would be bad ass."

"Language, young man. You better get a move on for first period."

"I can help you, you know, tell your adventures. Maybe we could make it a graphic novel."

"Let's first do the one we talked about a couple of weeks ago."

Emery cocked his head, his short dreads dangling to one side. "The one about the surfer? The Blaxican."

"Yeah, him, Gabaldón." The kid had come upon an article about Nick Gabaldón. In the 1940s when beaches were segregated here in the Southland, Gabaldón taught himself how to surf at a place called Inkwell Beach. It was a small slice of sand roped off for Black beachgoers in Santa Monica. He was of African American and Mexican heritage.

Once more Emery considered his answer. "Okay. But after we do that one then we can do the one about you." The warning bell rang, signaling it was five minutes before classes began.

"One step at a time," the bus driver said.

"You sound like my physical therapist" Emery was already walking away. He added, "Make sure you check the safety catch hooks."

"Every day, Em," Steptoe Biff said to his back. The soon-to-be teenager had an interest in mechanical engineering. Over his shoulder the youngster held up a thumb as he continued under the archways into the school.

No need to dwell on what Emery had said. One step at a time. He retrieved his tool kit kept next to his seat. He walked around the bus examining the exterior as he did each morning after his dropoff. At the lift he checked the safety catch hooks as well as tightened various nuts and screws connecting the hydraulics to the platform and other parts of the mechanism. Satisfied, he returned the platform to its upright position, and closed and secured the rear doors. One of the other drivers approached.

"How about some bones Friday night?" Clarence Cooper said. He was divorced, Steptoe unmarried. Both in their fifties.

"Sure, your place?"

"Yeah, bring some brew, I'll have sandwich fixins' and chips. It'll be four of us. Seven o'clock."

"Dominos fo' sho'." They bumped fists. Cooper got in his long bus and piloted it back onto the roadway, heading to the facilities yard. There the vehicle would stay until he was back on in the afternoon. Steptoe also got behind the wheel of his bus, but only to guide it to the employee parking lot. The A bus was owned by the school. While both men were classified as part-time employees of the school district, Steptoe's other job kept him onsite.

He was also the handyman here at the Cushing-Price Advancement Academy, a charter school designed for middle schoolers with special needs. Those needs might be of a physical nature and/or learning hurdles such as attention deficit hyperactivity disorder. He knew Emery was diagnosed as being on the spectrum but high functioning. For sure the kid could be a pain, but he was bright and observant. Maybe a little too much so. He got busy on his tasks.

"Biff, can you see about the lights in the girls' downstairs bathroom?" the principal Anna Lee Stokes asked him late in the morning. She was a pleasant-faced thirtysomething Black woman who kept her numerous keys on a spiral coil around her wrist. Each day was a different color. Today's was lavender, matching her skirt.

Steptoe was on a ladder changing the filter of one of the air intake grates for the HVAC system. "Sure thing, Ms. Stokes."

The principal lingered a moment, regarding him. "You okay?"

"Just concentrating on my work, ma'am."

"If you say so."

The rest of his day was more of the usual, and he was glad for it. He knew when he was taking the kids home, Em would continue questioning him.

They weren't a minute away from school before Em leaned forward and whispered, "So you used to be a drug lord?"

"Who told you that?"

"Don't you remember, from the video game?"

"Which one, Em?" He tried to sound light, keep the tightness out of his voice. The bus came to a stop sign at Cowan Park. Several young men occupied the crosswalk, heading to the basketball court. One of them remarked, "Look here, my niggas, I'm about to get a triple-double on your country asses today." The kids giggled as the older ones moved on.

Emery stayed on track. "Gear Streets, Den of the Black Pearl."

"Damn," Steptoe mumbled.

"What?"

"How am I mentioned in the game? And should you be playing this?"

"It's just car chases and first-person shooting." He showed big teeth in a broad smile. "I made it to the den, but the mantis trap got me. I'll be ready for it next time."

"Em, focus please."

"Oh yeah. Well, when you're in the alley outside the den and figure out the sequence to push in the bricks to open the secret door, a pretty lady appears when you step inside. 'Cause you're now in this kind of place where they play card games."

"A casino."

"Right. She looks a little like that other lady who used to be on TV with the big hair."

Steptoe didn't know who he was going on about but encouraged him. "For sure." On he went, making his drop offs, while Em told him details about the game. But he was patient. Steptoe made a turn onto a residential street. He slowed at an address. "Home again, home again, Deb." He went out to the rear of the bus.

Waving, she said, "See you tomorrow, Emery." She guided her wheelchair from the bus onto a wooden ramp ascending to her house.

"See you," he said waving back. Once she was off, it was just the two of them as Steptoe took Emery to his apartment. He lived with his youngish grandmother in a part of town called the Flats. It was where Steptoe had been born and raised. Where he first started as a corner boy and clawed and connived, strong-armed and killed his way to being the top motherfuckin' gun. A hollow chuckle rumbled from inside his chest as he drove, reminiscing.

"The lady in the game tells you," Emery said as if there

had been no interruption, "a few things about what to look out for in the casino. Then this guy comes in and she says your name, your real name, Bernard Steptoe."

"Okay..."

"She says she's happy to see you out of the joint and how you used to be called Biff-Bam." He paused. "Were you called that because you were like a boxer? Dropping fools, biff, bam," he said with sound effects.

"Something like that."

"Oh, and a blimp flies by outside the window you're looking out of. You know what it says on the side in lights?"

"The world is yours, " he said, staring out the windshield.

"How'd you know that?"

"Lucky guess."

"Anyway, once I heard that I looked you up. Saw your picture and everything. You knew a lot of pretty ladies when you were young, huh?"

One of them shot me. But he kept that to himself. "I suppose."

"Think I'll get to know some pretty ladies?" the kid asked.

"Slow your roll, playboy." He knew Emery would be thirteen soon. "Listen, this business about who I was. It's a secret between you and me, okay?"

"Right," Em beamed, nodding vigorously. "My lips are sealed."

"My man."

When he first got out, Steptoe had spent money he could ill afford to waste for a service that removed your presence from search engines and data brokers. But as the video game demonstrated, having once been a notorious cocaine kingpin lauded about in gangsta rap songs in his day, there was no escaping his past.

The following afternoon he greeted Em and his other regulars as they boarded the bus. Em was uncharacteristically quiet sitting behind him as he rode along.

"How was school today, Em?"

"It was okay." He looked off through the window.

"Everything all right at home?"

Emery kept mum and Steptoe didn't press him. After he dropped off his charges, he went back to the school and parked the bus for the evening. He left again in his car, an eight-year-old Mitsubishi Mirage he'd bought on a payment plan from a CarMax lot. He stopped to get gas. Playing on the pump-top display monitor was an ad for the "Best of Yo!" MTV Raps CD set. All of a sudden the damn '90s were in full effect, he reflected. Next Steptoe drove to the Ralphs supermarket near his house, going past the now fenced-off Alabama strip mall.

The Ralphs was part of a much larger open-air mall, an assortment of chain stores and mom-and-pop operations like Hu's Palace, which offered kung pao chicken with jalapenos. He made a few purchases. He was putting his bags in the Mirage's trunk when a car rolled into place behind him. Steptoe looked over his shoulder as the driver's window came down. His breath caught in his throat. He wasn't strapped. Steptoe'd been blasted before, though maybe this time he wouldn't see another twenty-four.

"How you doing?" The older Black man behind the wheel nodded cordially, a toothpick dangling from his mouth. What remained of his grey hair was cut short.

"Fine, officer, how are you?"

"Still got your ghetto radar working, don't you, Biff-Bam?"

"We know each other?" He closed the trunk and, folding his arms, leaned against the back of his car.

"Not really," the cop said. "But when I was walking a beat around here, we all knew about you. How you used tunnels and warrens to move your product before the cartels did that. Made sure to give out turkeys and hams with all the trimmings for the holidays. Money for kids heading to college. 'Course that was after they mamas got wrecked, becoming strawberries on the shit you peddled."

A tight smile on his face, the cop continued, "Time passes, right? Then what do you know, coming over here the other night for my chow mein and fried shrimp, thought I saw you dipping out of the drug store. And dammit, here you are."

Steptoe remained still.

"Lookin' to make a comeback like MJ when we was young?"

Finally, Steptoe said, "Nice catching up with you."

"See you around, big pimpin.' "

The window went up and Steptoe watched him go.

The following day, Emery wasn't waiting for him downstairs from his apartment. He called the kid's number and didn't get an answer. Steptoe shut off the bus and said, "Be right back. Everybody stay where they are."

"Okay, Mister Biff," Deb answered. "I'll keep everyone in line."

The rule was: no response, get on with it. Nonetheless, up Steptoe went to the second-floor breezeway leading to Emery's apartment. It was a home he shared with his grandmother Ivy Potts.

He knocked on the door and said, "Em, it's Biff, time for school." No answer. He resumed knocking, more insistent this time. Once more, no response. Back down at his bus, he glanced at the door as he started the engine and headed to school. Later, as he finished replacing a cartridge in a faucet in the cafeteria, Principal Stokes approached him.

"Did you see Emery this morning?" Stokes asked.

He told her what had happened. "What's up?"

"I called his grandmother's phone a couple of times and it went to voice mail. I left messages but no response." She kept her gaze on him. "The emergency contact number we have on file is disconnected."

"You want me to go over there now?" Absently, he put the pliers in his back pocket.

"Would you?"

"Of course."

Walking along a hallway toward the parking lot, from an open doorway up ahead came, "If I don't six, ain't a Je-zus!" A burst of oohs and laughter boomed as the familiar sound of dice clacking echoed from within.

Steptoe grinned. It was the Floating Castle Club, kids who got together during independent study time once a week to play board games with multi-sided dice. Doing battle against talking fire-breathing dragons and four-armed elves. He wagged his finger in the doorway at the dice thrower, Deb, gathered around a table with the other players.

"Sorry, Mr. Biff," she said sheepishly. "My grandpa was playing a Richard Pryor record last night."

"In his room, no doubt, and not for your ears, young lady."

"Mom said that, too."

At least their dice games didn't result in stabbings and shootings like his used to. He returned to Emery's apartment.

"Hey, hello," he said loudly, knocking on the door to no

avail. Two more tries, two more non-responses. Downstairs on the walkway a car pulled up. This time he didn't tense.

"Biff," Emery's grandmother, Ivy Potts, said to him from the passenger side of the car. She exited the idling vehicle, leaving the passenger side door open. There was another woman at the wheel. Potts was in her forties, lean with an unlined face. These days she kept her bronze-colored hair short. She was dressed in Dickies work pants and a matching shirt.

"Where's Em?" he asked, noting her red-rimmed eyes.

"I been out since early this morning looking for him. We circled back, just in case he showed up here."

"I knocked but didn't get an answer."

Bending down she looked back at the other woman. "Be right back, Tish."

"Okay."

She went past Steptoe and up the steps. He followed. Keying the lock she entered the apartment, revealing modest furnishing, no dishes piled in the sink.

Potts called out, "Em, you here?" She looked into rooms along a short hallway and returned.

Hands on his hips, Steptoe said, "He just slipped out last night while you were doing... what?" He glanced around but saw no evidence of the chronic. He knew she smoked. She thought it was on the QT, but Emery had told him.

"It's not like that." She rubbed a hand on her face. "I got a new job since the Jamba Juice closed down. My shift, though, is seven to two a.m. at the Teriyaki Donut."

"The all-night one on Sinnott?"

"Yeah. I always prepare dinner for Em before I leave, and he knows not to be answering the door if I'm not here. He's not slow... guess your boss would say I'm using the wrong word. But you know what I mean, Biff. He's just, him, listening to his own beat," she said proudly. "When I got home I figured he was asleep. I was tired and went to bed myself."

"But you got up?"

Back of her hand to her mouth, she yawned, saying, "'Round five some fools were out on the street, high, drunk, whatever, hittin' them switches like we used to do." She gave him a look and held up twin fingers. "Two 6-4 whips, bouncing up and down, doing donuts, blasting God knows what kind of rap from speakers the size of tiger shipping crates it sounded like."

"You must be gettin' old," he jibbed.

"Who you tellin,'" she answered straight-faced. "Anyway, they thankfully moved on and I went in to check on Em and saw he wasn't there, hadn't been to bed." She sat heavily on the arm of the couch, spreading her hands. "It's not like him to wander off. Even when we go out to the store or wherever and something attracts his attention, he'll ask me first if he can go take a look."

"What about a friend's house?" He was wondering if Emery went to play Deadly Street with someone.

Her face clouded. "His friends are from school, Biff. If he showed up at one of their places, a parent would have called me."

"Principal Stokes called you more than once."

She zeroed him with a look. "I get to talkin' to her and she gets that accusing tone in her voice with me," she stated. "Last year she damn near sicced children services on me." Ivy got up again. "I just have to find him."

"I'll help."

"I have to ask, 'cause I know it's in the back of your mind. You figure this has to do with you? Who you used to be?"

"But why take him if they wanted to get to me?" he said.

"To bargain," she answered flatly.

Long the rumors had persisted. When he finally got busted by a joint DEA and Sheriff's task force, there the authorities had been, on television, wheeling out dollies of cardboard boxes brimming with cash for all to see. Steptoe'd had his swag in more than one stash house. The law had cleaned him out. Even established that his various businesses were bought with illegally obtained monies and therefore were confiscated. More than once he'd come close to losing his life in prison over an inmate and his homies looking to hem Steptoe up — torture it out of him where he'd hidden his loot.

"Urban legends don't die, they only intensify," he noted grimily.

"Em can't be made to pay the price for our wrongs," she declared.

"I know."

More than twenty-five years ago, the two had met. Steptoe the high roller and Potts the not-quite-legal stripper at Jory's Juke in the Box, a strip club bordering the Flats where the hustlers made it rain and snow for the girls. They weren't romantically linked. But his money and fame was pull and she wanted to be a baller, too. She and her friends provided more than just a lap dance to his kind beyond the thrills of the VIP room. The two hadn't seen each other since then until Emery came to the school.

Steptoe asked, "He have his iPad with him?"

"He does. I sent him a few messages through his school app, nada."

"We need to get on back out there."

They both looked at Tish standing in the doorway. She was in jeans, curvy and toned. Steptoe blinked hard.

"Yeah, negro, you know me."

Tish had also been a dancer at Jory's. He also remembered she used to go around with one of his rivals.

"Guess it would be foolish of me to ask to tag along."

"Please," Tish answered, dismissing him with a wave of her hand. "Nobody needs your triflin' ass tryin' to boss us around."

Potts put a hand on his arm. "You find Em, you better call me."

"Of course." The three left the apartment. Back in his car, Steptoe called Principal Stokes. First he advised her to get a substitute to drive his bus this afternoon.

"If you can't find him today," she was saying, "I'm duty-bound to get the district involved. They get involved, I have to tell them about you, your record. A missing special needs child will bring attention."

"I understand, Anna Lee. You'll have to do what's necessary to save the school."

"This school means so much, Biff, not just to me, but students like Emery."

"I'll do my damnedest."

Steptoe started the car, but didn't put it in gear. Assuming Emery had left his apartment of his own volition, what would be his purpose? It had to have something to do with Emery's current fixation on learning about his past. Had Emery's hormones kicked in and he went in search of a pretty lady for himself? Putting the transmission in drive, Steptoe headed to his next destination.

His kids lived in different areas of town. This meant the bus took them past all sorts of sights. Lately on the back end of Cowan Park, several RVs had begun to show up, signaling those inside were unhoused. They parked where they could until such time as complaints from residents brought the police.

"I like her robe," Deb had said the other week when their bus went past the RVs.

Steptoe and everyone else looked to see a white woman of a certain age with frizzed out brown-blonde hair step out of an RV. She wore a short terrycloth robe and was lighting a cigarette. There was a bright green alligator embroidered on the upper part of the robe. An older man also stepped out in a suit, tucking in his shirt.

"Do they live there, Mister Biff?" she'd asked.

"Must be, Deb."

Emery, though, had displayed a crooked smile he'd noted in the rearview. It wasn't long before Steptoe was knocking on the door of the RV where he'd seen the alligator woman previously exit. A big rig was parked not far away. He knew her vehicle from the others as it had a square of cardboard taped in place over a broken-out window. The door creaked opened.

"What can I do for you, rugged and smokey?" she said, appraising him. The woman held a lit cigarette and an energy drink in one hand, wearing jean shorts — Daisy Dukes they called them in his day — and a loose t-shirt with the faded words MIND YOUR MANNERS on it.

"Want to know if you've seen this kid?" He held up his phone showing a photo of a grinning Emery in a top hat. It had been taken on the occasion of the school's Christmas play.

"He your son?"

"No. He's my good buddy though."

"Then come back later," a man said from inside.

Turning her head sideways she said, "Be cool, Brian."

"I got to get back on the road. You out here playing hostess and shit. I'm paying good money here, ain't I?"

"So am I for the right information," Steptoe said, also raising his voice.

Heavy steps, then Brian appeared. He was white, in his late forties, and beefy. He'd already stripped down to his t-shirt but still had on his requisite trucker's cap. "Look, dude," Brian began, pointing at Steptoe's phone showing Em and his crutch, "Kimmy says she ain't seen your little crippled buddy. So get to getting." As he said this, he pushed past the woman to glare down at Steptoe.

"Ableist motherfuckah." Steptoe snatched him by his t-shirt and pulled him out of the RV, stepping aside as the trucker struck the ground.

"Hey, goddammit," Brain wailed, starting to get up.

Steptoe slammed the bottom of his foot into his chest, causing the larger man to wheeze and gag as he was put down again. Steptoe grabbed his crotch with the pliers he'd brought along.

"Oh, man, please," Brian pleaded, trying to scoot away as Steptoe applied pressure.

"I'm'a squeeze them off if you blink, bitch. Back when, I would've unloaded my AK on you for your discourteousness."

"Hey, hold on," Kimmy said, chuckling, coughing and spitting. "Damn."

She had a hand on Steptoe's shoulder. "Ease up, honey, he don't mean what he says." She dug her fingers into his muscle. "I saw the kid way early this morning."

"You talked to him?" Steptoe said, straightening up. Brian got off the ground and went back inside the RV.

Kimmy blew smoke from her cigarette. "I happened to be up early and when I looked out, he was there, leaning on his crutch looking over here." She pointed toward a green patch of the park. "I think he was thinking about knocking on my door." She held up a hand at Steptoe's look. "I wasn't for one second considering anything like what's on your dirty mind. I did get on some clothes though but when I got the door open, he was walking off that way." This time she pointed toward the residential section.

There was an around-the-clock 7-Eleven a few blocks in that direction, Steptoe knew from his route. He'd turned to walk away. Kimmy put a hand on his arm and brought her face close to the side of his. She smelled strongly of nicotine and caffeine.

"When you find the kid, come on back and we'll celebrate. I bet you know how to run it deep, baby."

At the 7-Eleven, he showed the bored clerk, a tatted young Latinx woman, Emery's picture.

"Sure, I know Em," she said.

"How do you know him?"

"My sister went to Cushing-Price. She has a spine thing."

"Could he be visiting her?"

"She's upstate at college now."

"Was he here earlier?"

"Yeah, he was," she said, as if only now realizing something. "Usually, he comes by in the afternoons to buy a hot dog and Doritos." She rang up a purchase and fixed Steptoe with a look. "You're the bus driver."

"That's right. Now wait a minute, we're like four miles from his house. Does he come here with his grandmother?"

"Naw, most times he flies in on a Bird."

For a moment he was confused. When he was Biff-Bam, a bird was slang for a kilo of coke. "You're talking about one of those e-scooters?"

"Hm-hmm."

"He don't have a driver license."

She cocked her head at him and snorted. "Like it's hard

to get around that."

"Was he on a scooter this morning?"

"Walking, I think. He told me he walks to build up his muscles. We chit-chatted a bit, asking me about Simy, that's my sister, and then he left."

"Where'd he go?"

She shrugged. "School, I figured. He likes it there."

Hand rubbing the back of his neck, despair was a stone in Steptoe's stomach. "When he comes by here in the afternoons, is there anybody else he knows in the neighborhood? Anybody. I've got to find him."

"He's missing?" she said.

"And I gotta find him."

"I'll call my sister, okay? She knows him, she might be helpful."

"Please do." They exchanged cell numbers.

Back outside, a public bus was pulling away from a bus stop. On the front of the bus the digital crawl on the destination sign announced its further stops as it headed west to the beach. "Huh," he said, an idea forming. Off he went and got to the abandoned Alabam strip mall.

Years ago before the strip mall existed, Jory's was located here. He parked and, as he hoped, found a slit in the chain link fencing around the whole of it. Several pup tents and assorted items were camped inside. A sign, like Kimmy's RV, that the unhoused found a home wherever they could land — if only temporarily. More than one pup tent was outfitted with an extension cord. A heavy-duty one led into here from the base of an old-fashioned light post nearby on the sidewalk, a TA panel at the base covering its wiring having been removed. Walking toward what was once the Surf Wind, he heard a rhythmic whirring from within. The business, where customers once could ride artificially produced, waves, had been boarded up. But one of the plywood panels had been removed in the rear of the structure. He went in.

The words heavy in his throat, he said, "Em, you know how worried you had us?"

"I wanted to do this and not have you or grandma or Miss Anna tell me not to." The young man was holding onto the railings of one of the two surf simulators he apparently had been tinkering with since before daylight. He'd removed a lower covering in the machine to get to the motor. Tools and such were spread about on the floor. His crutch, too, lay aside. The simulator was built something like a treadmill, but instead of a track, there was an oblong platform to stand on and ride at different speeds when in motion. The machine was plugged into a lengthy extension cord trailing out of the building. Surf Wind had advertised a cool and different way to work out. Once there had been a row of these machines. Why these two were left, even if they weren't operational, wasn't clear. There was nothing else inside.

"How'd you know these were still in here?"

"After we talked about Gabaldón I remembered this place. I came by then and I've been back a couple of other times. Renny let me hook up to the power."

He figured Renny was one of the homeless folks. Sighing, he said, "You might as well finish your ride."

"Okay, Biff, then you can go next."

"And break my hip?"

Em turned a dial on the control board, upping his speed some. He gripped the railing on either side, leaning forward. He went up-and-down, and side-to-side in a set pattern. All the while, his eyes envisioning a big wave he rode like Gabaldón. Steptoe took pictures of him, sending them along with a text to Ivy Potts.

That evening he and the principal had coffee in her office.

"You did good, unk. Today was a good day." Clinking her cup against his, she took a sip.

"If anything would have happened to Em, or any of those kids," Steptoe began, but didn't finish. He looked away, hiding his misting eyes.

"I know," she said quietly. "I feel the same way. About all of them."

No one at the Cushing-Price Advancement Academy knew these two were related. Out of the millions of Biff-Bam the Magic Man's seized monies, one specific amount had been successfully laundered. It was the seed funding he'd provided his special education-trained niece with to start the school.

They sat quietly, each to their own thoughts.

About the Author

The son of a mechanic and a librarian with roots in the Texas Hill Country and the Mississippi Delta, Gary Phillips must keep writing to forestall his appointment at the cross-roads. He's written novels, short stories, comic books, and was a staff writer on FX's *Snowfall*, about crack and the CIA in 1980s South Central. His latest novel *Ash Dark as Night* set against the 1965 Watts Riots, was named a best mystery last year by *Parade* magazine and *Publishers Weekly*."Biff-Bam, The Magic Man" was inspired by Ice Cube's "It Was a Good Day."

GRAMMA'S HEART

VICKI HENDRICKS

THE TOAST POPS and I butter it. There's a rifle in the closet. I saw it when I got out my fluffy pink slippers this morning, the first cold day of fall. I want to think somebody gave the gun to Jeremy to store. I should get my phone from the back bedroom. I hear his footsteps coming downstairs.

I pull the warm plate from the oven and start piling up the scrambled eggs and heaping on the bacon. I smile and show a cheery face, but it doesn't register with him. Not much does, nothing happy, since his mom took off with a jockey in early summer. She called Jeremy twice, I think. His supposed father, my son, hasn't stopped by for months either, but I'm thinking Jer couldn't care less about that.

When Jeremy was little, he was my best buddy. We'd watch reruns of *Bugs Bunny* and laugh at how Elmer Fudd wasn't funny. When he was in eighth grade, I broke my ankle, and he played poker with me on Sunday afternoons to cheer me up. We bet with piles of peanuts and shared our winnings. I can smell those roasted peanuts. Seems like nothing's changed.

His eyes focus on my slippers as he crosses the room. They're almost neon. He knows where I keep them.

"Bacon's crunchy how you like it. Gram made the eggs as fluffy as clouds 'cause she loves you." He won't look at me. I want to reach up and grab him around the neck, hug him against my face, and give him a smacking kiss on the ear, like he used to let me do. Never let him go. He moves to the table, looking dazed. He's wearing the flannel shirt that makes his blue eyes blinding. I set the plate in front of him. He grunts.

"Did I hear a 'Thanks, Gram'?"

His eyes go to the bacon. I don't mean to antagonize him. I understand. He's so lonely, stuck in the boonies with me, no friends, nothing to do but hang out in the woods or play computer games with strangers all the way across the country. I was hoping he'd meet new people when school started. There's still a chance. It's only been a couple weeks. I thought he had a little girlfriend. I saw the name Shana, inside a fancy heart, on his sketchbook cover. But when I asked if he met any cute girls, he said, "Gramma, no girls like me." He stared at me like I should know that. I didn't want to hurt his feelings more, or be a nosy old gram, so I didn't say anything else.

I bring us each a cup of coffee and sit in the chair across from him. I put two spoons of sugar and a glug of milk into his. He sips, looking through me. When he sets down the cup, his face reminds me of the first morning I dropped him at kindergarten. His chin is pushed up, making his bottom lip stick out and creases run down the sides. Not many whiskers yet, but just like Gramps' chin when he was faced with a job he hated, like shoveling snow off the driveway. A job I should have stopped him from doing.

"Take a few bites for Gram. Got to eat a good breakfast. Never know what the day might bring."

My voice was shaky at the end. Being a whiny gramma isn't going to help anything — if anything can be helped. "Grease is brain food."

Somehow that spurs him into action and he picks up two pieces of bacon and crunches them down in seconds. He crams the other three pieces into his mouth before he has time to chew. A few crumbs fall out onto the plate.

His arm moves robot-like as he shovels the eggs into his mouth with a triangle of toast. He'll be out the door in no time. I can't leave him to get my phone. Tears leak out of my eyes. It's eating at me, my fear. I go to the sink and use my nails to scrape viciously at the white egg scum on the bottom of the cast iron skillet.

I glance at the back of his head, wavy brown hair all in place. He was born with a full head of hair. Over his shoulder I see his plate is empty. "More toast? Oh, I got us some blackberry jam. Only takes a second."

He scoots back his chair and heads toward the closet. Time starts to wink, or my mind's gone crazy, lighting him up, off and on, with gaps of black chopping up his movements, turning the flow of his legs into a skip, like an old movie when the film got stuck.

He opens the closet door partway and pulls out a backpack I didn't see. It's crammed full. I get dizzy, hunch over the sink, brace myself, and watch a soap bubble in the skillet, a rainbow sliding over it before it bursts. A hanger bangs in the closet and fabric rustles. The front door creaks open.

I turn, expecting the back of his quilted maroon jacket. He's staring at me, hardened anguish in his eyes, the backpack in one hand, the rifle in the other.

"I love you, Jeremy. I know. I know it isn't enough."

Tears follow his downturned mouth to his chin, drip off. "I love you, too, Gramma."

He slings the rifle belt onto his shoulder and lifts the backpack, looking like a soldier, my soldier. He snatches the car keys from the hook and pockets them. "I'm taking the car today."

"Jeremy!" Holding myself up against the sink, I clutch at a shooting pain in my chest. I gasp. "I think I'm having a heart attack. Jer?"

He blinks hard, then steps out onto the porch. The door stands open.

I'm running blind, the heavy skillet cocked behind my ear, wailing like a banshee, trusting my heart will last. I smash at his head, hating myself, hating the world, hating God.

The skillet bounces off his shoulder once, twice. I'm short and weak, betrayed by age. He flings me away and lets the backpack drop. Gripping a chair, pleading with my eyes, I work my way up to stand. His hands go expertly to the rifle, sliding back the black top piece, thumbing down the safety. His finger finds the trigger as he snugs the butt into his shoulder.

"Jeremy, who will get the lid off the blackberry jam, honey? Who'll reach the turkey platter? Sweetie?"

His face is red, drawn tight into a wad of pain, tears and snot running, like when little Lola had to be put down, not long ago. He lowers the gun and wipes his sleeve across his eyes.

"Jeremy, let's get a dog! This morning! I saw a sign on the road — eight weeks old, retriever pups. I don't care if I have to feed it and walk it and clean up its mess. Gram will do that for you. It doesn't matter anymore, honey. Nothing matters."

He raises the rifle. Faces of boys and girls flood my brain, young bodies draped on overturned desks.

Spatter thick as pitch hits the wall behind me. Relief. Almost joy.

About the Author

Vicki Hendricks is the author of noir novels *Miami Purity, Iguana Love, Voluntary Madness, Sky Blues,* and Edgar Award Finalist *Cruel Poetry*. Next, *Fur People* falls into the little-known category of animal-hoarder noir. Her unnatural short stories are collected in *Florida Gothic Stories*. *Chez Usher*, her newest novel, has been dubbed "gothic noir." After years of scuba, sailing, skydiving, and other research, she now gets her adrenaline rushes by trapping cats for TNR.

DOMESTIC

MIKE MCHONE

THE DAY after his wife's funeral, Walter Corrigan bought his first case of Coors Light in over twenty-two years. He left the 7-Eleven, went home, opened the first bottle, and when the beer hit his lips, a golden euphoria flooded his body. He sat in his recliner with his shoes on, drank one after the other, watched TV, left the newspaper on the floor, and got up only to piss and heat up a TV dinner in the microwave. By four p.m., he sank his sixth Coors and was good and buzzed. While a rerun of *Barney Miller* played on TV, he sat in his recliner and looked over at the couch and saw the image of his wife from four days prior at the end of the couch doing her cross-stitching. She was making... What was it? A snowman? Santa Claus? He couldn't remember. Five days ago she made a chicken dinner with mashed potatoes. It was the last homecooked meal he ate.

The sound of a laugh track filled the living room.

With his head delightfully woozy, he stood, walked to the bedroom, stripped to his underwear and took a nap. He woke at six that evening, went back to the living room in his t-shirt and boxers, and continued drinking. When he hit beer number twelve at nine that night, he watched himself — as if he were a fictional character in a story of his own design — rise out of his chair and make the first of two decisions he would never consciously undertake without the unintended resolve only alcohol can give a man.

First: He took an armful of Marion's clothes to the burn barrel behind his house, soaked the clothes with lighter fluid, tossed in a match, and stood in the cold September night watching the smoke rise to Heaven. The viewer part of himself felt guilty about what he'd done. The fictional part of him did not. After all, it was she who had decided to end their marriage of forty-eight years by way of a bottle of Xanex, and didn't leave a note, an explanation, a reason as to why she wanted to leave him, so... A few minutes passed (or maybe it was hours, he didn't know) and Walter grabbed the garden hose, doused the flames, and went back inside.

Second: He stumbled past the TV, grabbed another beer along his route, went to the computer room, got on the internet, and ordered a sex doll.

He finished the beer, went to sleep, and didn't dream.

It arrived three weeks later. The shipping company had set the wooden crate at the foot of his driveway. Walter, spying for neighbors, hurried, took a handcart, and wheeled the crate inside his garage. He turned on the light, closed the garage door, took a screwdriver and hammer, and pried open the crate. It was there beneath the bubble wrap. It wasn't a cheap doll, or a blow-up doll, the kind you'd get as a gag gift for a bachelor party, but rather a realistic one with synthetic skin and features that, although exaggerated in the breasts and hips, looked human. Walter removed the bubble wrap and... There she was. Her eyes, sapphire blue and open, thick lips, tan skin, massive tits, black hair cut in the style of a 1950s pinup. It was naked and looked (what was the word?) vulnerable. The website gave customers the option to order clothes along with the doll, sexy lingerie, a corset and the like, but Walter didn't see the point considering she wasn't a real woman and it made as much sense as putting a Barbie outfit on a hand.

In that moment, he remembered Marion watching a reality TV show a couple years ago about people with unusual addictions. Whatever the show was called, one episode focused on a guy that lived with a Real Doll and treated the doll as if it was his wife or girlfriend, bought it clothes and jewelry, celebrated anniversaries and everything like a normal couple. "What kind of pervert does that?" Marion asked. Walter replied with a "Yeah," and checked a website on his phone a few minutes after she'd gone to bed that night to see how much one would cost. He found they ran anywhere from a thousand to ten-thousand dollars depending on the features, add-ons, and accessories. He told himself at the time only a freak would spend that much money on a masturbatory aide, but in the long hours after he found Marion's body and she was taken away to the coroner, he found himself remembering all those stories he'd overheard in the lunchroom at work from the guys and their trips to strip clubs or Chinese massage parlors, and came to the conclusion that, really, it wasn't any different. Whether you pay a human being or buy a device, the end result is always the same. However, unlike his former coworkers, he could sleep at night knowing at least he was never unfaithful to his wife, even now.

Walter took a metal folding chair off the pegboard on the wall of the garage and placed it in the center of the garage. He pulled the doll out of the box and was surprised at the weight of it, somewhere around sixty or seventy pounds, he figured. He dragged it over to the folding chair and sat it down.

The doll looked at him. Walter stood before it, his eyes taking in every inch, the curvature of the eyebrows, the thickness of the eyelashes, the neck, the breasts, the nipples, the belly button, waist, thighs, feet, toes. His heart raced. Sweat rose. A charged nervousness drafted through every extremity, and a stirring he hadn't felt in years, welled inside him in that secret space just below the heart, just above the gut. The doll was beautiful. The doll was perfect.

Walter brushed his fingertips against its cheek. His hands ran through the hair, slid down its shoulders and arms. He leaned in and kissed the doll on the mouth. Although it didn't move, it felt... It felt real. So real.

He shoved his tongue into the mouth and his hands latched onto the breasts for a moment before they made their way up her body and found the throat. Walter caressed the throat, sighed, blinked, then squeezed gently. He pulled his mouth away, squeezed harder and felt the metallic rod beneath the synthetic skin, and felt, too, the padding give just a little with the pressure. He stared into its eyes, pulled his right hand away while his left fixed itself on the center of the neck. He opened his right hand, brought it down, and slapped the doll across the cheek. The eyes never flinched. He slapped it again. The look stayed. Another slap. He choked harder. He felt the warm sting of arthritis flare up in his hands and elbows, but he ignored it. It didn't matter. He pulled her hair, brought his hand back, slapped her again, choked harder.

His thoughts turned to a young woman he'd seen in a movie he'd watched on his phone years prior. He'd never seen a woman get slapped in a film before and had never had any inclination to search out such a thing. The only reason he decided to watch that particular film was because the screen capture on the porn site featured an incredibly endowed woman. The slap across her face came after her male costar had stripped her bare and laid her down on a bed. Walter never expected to see such a thing, never even dreamed of it, but when it happened, he thought of it multiple times a week, every week until that day in the garage. Certainly, he would never have asked Marion if she would consider trying it. She was a quiet, proper woman and wouldn't tolerate it, he assumed. Besides, she was, like him, old and they hadn't had relations in the years prior to her death, so why bring it up at all?

Walter wrapped both hands around the doll's throat and throttled it. Its eyes locked onto him, now, it seemed, with a look of shock.

He stopped. He stepped back. The excitement inside him faded along with the flare-ups in all parts of his body.

He swiped a hand across his forehead and wiped his palms on his pant legs. He turned out the light and went inside.

They'd gotten married a month after they'd graduated high school and tried for a child the night of the wedding. After six months without any luck, Walter urged Marion to see a doctor. She made an appointment for the following week and, after the visit, she told Watler the doctor informed her it would be incredibly difficult for her to conceive. "Why?" he asked.

"He said it could be a lot of things," she told him. "Ovulation problems, hormones."

"What are you going to do?"

"I guess we can keep trying," she said.

Not long after, over Christmas dinner, Walter's parents asked when they could expect a grandchild. "Hopefully soon," he said. They believed him and it was a blessing that they were killed in a carbon monoxide leak the following year because he never had to disappoint them again. Marion never said whether or not his in-laws pressed her about a child, and he never asked, not wanting to upset her.

The last time he held a bat was in high school.

He thought back to the last game of the regular season. Coleman High faced off against Burton Senior High and Dickey Morris was on the mound. Burton was a pack of bastards anyway, and Coleman had never beaten them in the three years Walter had been on the team. Burton's star player, Dickey Morris, was a pro in a high schooler's uniform. The guy had a Howitzer for an arm and his two-seam fastball could rival Bob Gibson's. Walter knew when he took the plate it was only a matter of three, maybe four or five throws, if he was lucky, before he was out.

It was the top of the second inning and Coleman was already down 2-0. Morris threw the first pitch. It flew by Walter like a bullet. The second came. Swing. Miss. With the third, he connected, but it ended up a popup fly the catcher caught without much effort.

He faced down Morris twice more that evening, and he struck out each time — as did half the dugout. The closing pitcher came in at the eighth, did just as good of a job as Morris, and the slaughter lasted until the bottom of the ninth. The game ended 10-0. It was like a group of tee ballers had faced off against the Yankees. And it wasn't like Coleman was a gaggle of shit birds. They were good, but there was something about Burton High, and Dickey Morris especially.

As he held the bat, memories of Dickey Morris seeped out of the wood like sap. His arthritis flared when he swung the bat and connected with the right side of the doll's head, but he ignored the pain. The doll leaned to the left after he hit it and started to slip, so he hit it again, this time on the left side.

Walter was ambidextrous and he was able to bat both left and right. It helped him in school, but, of course, it didn't do much for him in the real world. It's not like he was going to write up monthly reports any faster in the office of Garland Manufacturing. Yeah, there was that one time he mentioned he could bat both left and right to a coworker, a guy named Gus Shaker who worked with him in the logistics department. Gus, a baseball fanatic, looked surprised when Walter mentioned his hidden talent. "Never figured you for an athlete," he said.

"Well, I was," Walter said.

"I know, but, you know, you don't lookit."

"Well, I was, I said." Walter said nothing more and went back to work.

He brought the bat down on top of the doll's head, right where the fontanelle would've been.

Garland was a good place. He got in right out of high school, worked his way up from the factory floor to the office, and stayed there until he retired at sixty-two with a nice pension and enough in the bank to last him the rest of his life. The place had good insurance and plenty of vacation time.

He stood to the side and hit the doll in the face, right on the bridge of the nose. He pulled the bat back and struck it again in the mouth. Again, in the forehead. Again, in the stomach.

He even got to use a company car.

Again, in the forehead. Again, in the stomach.

He also got a bonus every year at Christmas.

His elbows felt like they'd been dipped in magma. Walter put the bat back into the little green chest with his mitt, a little hard plastic box filled with baseball cards, and his old uniform. He closed the lid, shoved it back under the workbench, and moved the lawnmower back to where it was in front of the chest.

There was a group of five or six old men that would hang out at McDonald's every morning. Sometimes he'd head down there, usually after eating at the diner, and sit with them for an hour or two. He didn't mind it most days. It was good when they talked about the Tigers or the White Sox or a new show they saw on television. He didn't even mind it when the talk steered toward politics or religion, considering the men believed and voted the same, but when one of them started in on talking about pains they were having, or families, or what they did in Vietnam, Walter would make up an excuse to head home. New shows or a recent game were good to talk about. Hearing the same stories about this or that ailment, or this surgery so-and-so needed, or that funeral, or something somebody did a long time ago bored him. He never met the men's families or coworkers or old military buddies or spouses, and he didn't want to hear Stan utter the same complaints about not being to run as fast as he used to, or listen to Robert talk about how his knees and ankles hurt all the time, or sit through the same story about the time Jerry was in the middle of a firefight in 'Nam and how he "was scared half to death." Walter had his own ailments and he never served in the war, so what did this have to do with him? When that nonsense came up, he'd gulp down his coffee, say something like, "Well, I better get started on the lawn," or "I need to take a look at that sump pump," or something of the sort and duck out and wonder all the way home why he kept going back there week after week, seeing the same faces over and over again.

And how did it start? A week after he retired, he went to McDonald's around six in the morning to grab some breakfast. Marion was still asleep at that time and would probably lie in bed for another two or three hours. He'd always been an early riser and Marion always slept in. He didn't realize how long she'd stay in bed until that first week he didn't have to go to work. She usually turned in at nine and sometimes didn't get up until nine or ten the next day, then she'd nap around one or two, sometimes five. She never wanted breakfast and would get irritated when Walter would wake her up and ask. "No," she'd snap. "Just let me sleep." Not wanting to disturb her, he headed out to get a McMuffin and some coffee.

When he walked in, he saw Gus Shaker sitting there with some other guys about their age. Gus called him over, invited him to sit down, and that was that. He started going there once, twice, sometimes three times a week, and kept going after Gus died. By that point, he assumed they were all friends. He never asked how all the rest of them met each other but they spoke as if they'd known each other their entire lives, and maybe they had.

One morning, after he'd taken a blowtorch and burned the doll's tits off, Stan mentioned Robert had passed away. "Cancer," was all he said and didn't specify what kind. "Funeral's at Smith Brothers at nine, Tuesday morning, but they're having a showing on Monday afternoon at five or six."

Stan and Jerry talked about Robert, while Doug, the oldest of the group at seventy-eight, sat quietly. Walter finished his coffee, told them he'd see them at the funeral home, and headed out because he had a doctor's appointment that morning.

He went to the showing but skipped the funeral. He ordered flowers though.

Bukkake.

Such a strange word. He didn't know what it meant. Then he clicked on a video he found online and saw the definition.

He imagined himself and the guys from McDonald's in his garage for a moment but pushed the thought away and cleaned up.

Marion never came out and said that she didn't like him drinking so much, but she made her disgust known one morning about twenty-six years or so after they'd taken their vows. Walter woke up on a Saturday morning after he'd spent a Friday night plowing down a case of beer and heard the sound of breaking glass. He walked out into the living room, eyes blurry, head like a block of soft concrete, and he saw her with a trash bag in one hand, empty beer bottle in the other, and a tired, drawn look on her face. "Good morning," he said, and she replied, "It'd be nice if you'd pick up after yourself," then tossed the beer bottle into the bag. "This is getting old," she'd said. "Sorry," he told her. "That's what you said last week, and the week before that, and the week before that." He almost apologized again, but when the sound of another broken bottle blasted into the room, he ran to the bathroom to vomit.

He tried to convince himself throughout the rest of the day that his drinking wasn't that bad, that he wasn't a full-blown alcoholic, and he only relegated it to once a week. He knew a guy at his work, a guy named Charlie Delain, who ran his wife off with his drinking. He wrecked a few cars, got a few DUIs, and came home to find her gone. She left a note that said she took the kids and moved back with her mother. Divorce papers were mailed to him a couple weeks later. By that point, Charlie had started drinking morning, noon, and night, and when he showed up for his shift in the shipping and receiving department the day after getting the divorce papers, he got on a hi-lo, hit the gas, and ran the thing directly into a packaging machine. He ran over a coworker's foot and ended up doing about three grand in damage to the machine. The only reason Walter knew anything about Charlie's home situation at all was because when he went down to the shop floor to see what was going on, he found Charlie on the ground crying his eyes out, saying what his wife had done, how he missed his kids, how he regretted everything. Charlie got up and tried to apologize to the coworker with the demolished foot but the only thing that came out of his mouth was drool and gibberish. Walter called an ambulance and the cops then spent the rest of his shift filing out incident reports and insurance paperwork.

"At least I'm not as bad as that idiot," Walter told himself, but in the particular type of sobering moment only a severe hangover can bestow upon an individual, he realized he was only a few more cases of beer away from getting too damn close to the vicinity of Charlie. He didn't want that for himself, so he declared that morning he'd never touch another drink again. She said, "We'll see," and he held to his promise for twenty-two years, and even though he'd started drinking again, could it really be considered a broken promise if she was dead?

Impossible to know.

The day after Robert's showing, he polished off a case of Coors by the time six p.m. rolled around then started in on a fifth of rum. He made about two rum and Coke's before he passed out.

His last remembered thought of the night, right before the rum joined forces with the beer in his system, was, "She never left *me* a note."

The tongue was equipped with a vibration device. The website encouraged patrons to slather the tongue in lubricant, turn on the device, and enjoy the sensation. It was interesting, Walter thought, when he plucked the tongue out of her mouth with a pair of pliers. Interesting to see the black hole in the center of her face, just above the charred chest, just below the smashed nose.

He went to work on the eyes next, and what was once a face, now looked like a Halloween mask fixed onto a ravaged mannequin. He took the blowtorch and singed off her hair, face, and skin on the rest of her body, and the finality disgusted him.

He cleaned up the creamy, hardened pool of melted skin, deposited it into a trash bag, and took the pliers and a screwdriver then disassembled the metallic skeleton, dumped them in the recycle bin, and set her remains out to the curb.

"When we walk with Christ..."

As much as he wanted to, he couldn't focus on the sermon that Sunday morning. He thought, instead, of how she had looked when she was taken apart, how the flesh and hair smelled when it was burned from her body, the sounds her skeleton made as it rattled in the recycle bin as he dragged it to the curb. He also thought of Marion's body.

Walter had come home that morning after breakfast at the diner and found her on the floor of the bedroom. He checked for a pulse the way they do on TV and found nothing but cold flesh. He called 911 and as he paced the floor, wondering what questions they'd ask him, he saw the prescription medication bottle on the floor next to the nightstand. Walter picked it up and read the words "Xanex" and "Dr. Kati." He knew what Xanex was, but he'd never heard of this Dr. Kati. After the police came and the medical examiner's office hauled her body away, he looked up who Dr. Kati was and found out she was a psychiatrist.

The police asked him the same questions he'd asked himself on occasion since that day. Was she depressed? Did she give any clue that she wanted to end her life? Were there signs? He was honest with them and himself when he answered no repeatedly. He thought of talking to Dr. Kati, but he figured she would invoke doctor/patient confidentiality, or whatever they called it on the cop shows Marion used to watch.

"We need to uplift each other, and..."

Why hadn't she said anything? They'd been together for nearly fifty years. Fifty, for God's sake. They'd taken a vow. Sickness, health, rich, poor. It would've been easy for her to talk to him, to say anything, to tell him anything, to share anything, any of her innermost secrets and thoughts and ideas and problems. She was his wife, his girl, his baby, as he called her. Why wouldn't she tell him anything? Why couldn't she have just...

"Let us pray... Heavenly Father..."

He ordered another doll and the end results were the same as the previous one with the exception that he died before he had a chance to burn the flesh and hair away.

On the morning of his last day, Walter went out to the garage after sinking six beers and went to work throttling the doll. But this time, afterward, he decided to lay her on the floor and try out the vibrating tongue. During his climax, he felt an explosion in his chest. His knees buckled and he felt face-first onto the concrete, his member still planted firmly in the doll's mouth.

It took six weeks for his body to be found, and that was only after his neighbor had returned home from a month-long vacation in Florida and noticed an awful smell coming from the Corrigan property. By that point, decomposition had set in and what the police found looked like a pile of brown-yellow sludge coating a sex doll. They drew their conclusions as to what took place and made jokes about it in private.

Since Walter had no heirs, no will, or locatable living relatives, the county took possession of the house, cleaned it out, and put it up for sale. They'd tossed out Walter's pornography collection, of course, and went through the numerous boxes and totes in the basement. While one worker dug through a tote of Halloween decorations they came across a long-since-expired container of birth control pills. They tossed the pills into the trash along with the pornography and the sex doll.

Walter's remains were sent to Smith Brothers Funeral Home, where they were cremated, tossed away, and taken to the county landfill. The house was eventually sold to a young couple from Cincinnati with two little girls, a calico cat named Cheshire, and a Scottish terrier named Izzy.

The neighbors said they seemed like nice, ordinary people.

About the Author

Mike McHone's work has appeared in *Dark Yonder, Ellery Queen's Mystery Magazine, Alfred Hitchcock's Mystery Magazine, Guilty, Rock and a Hard Place,* the Anthony Award-nominated anthology *Under the Thumb: Stories of Police Oppression* edited by SA Cosby, and elsewhere. Learn more about the author at mikemchone.com, or find him on Instagram: @mike_mchone.

BENNY THE BOOSTER & CHLAMYDIA JANE

JON HORN

We were enjoying a hot cup of joe at the Turk's (he's really Lebanese but everyone calls him "the Turk"), whose diner we regularly patronize as it's close to the House and also because the Turk, a cop buff, never lets us pay for our coffee-and. Of course in these reformed times cops aren't "on the pad" anymore, but we still get our little perks and freebies here and there, like snacks on the arm at the Turk's. We never order big, mind you. We like the Turk and we want him to stay in business. And the way the Turk figures, it's no big deal to comp our table. If his place is known as a PD hangout, he needn't worry about deadbeats or stickups.

As usual we were talking shop, and this week the big buzz on the blue grapevine was all about two city cops. One, in a precinct across town, had just been "constructively terminated" — in other words he had to quit before he was fired — because he was found, and not for the first time, getting a hot BJ from a street hooker in the backseat of his cruiser. This guy was known to put the moves on civilian babes, there'd been complaints, and now his PC put it to him: leave the force voluntarily or be brought up on charges and disgraced. He went quietly. And he got no sympathy from our table at the Turk's. Sure, any one of us might take a piece of tail in trade once in a while — but a cunthound cop not only embarrassed the Department, he might also be too busy chasing pussy when you needed backup fast. Fuck the horny shmuck! A guy had to know when and where to use his tool, and it wasn't too cool to do so on the job, at least not as a rule.

We were also talking about a cop across the river who freaked out, killed his wife, then ate his gun. It happens. The daily pressures on cops are greater than on most civilians. And the option of deadly force is always at hand. But the guys coffeeing up at the Turk's didn't have any good words for this cop either. A cop who couldn't control his feelings, who used his service weapon on his wife and then himself — well, DDT (Detective Darrel Troy) said it best, using one of his favorite expressions: "That guy must have been a sorry scrap of scrotum."

Then an old uniform came into the diner and sat with us, a weary look on his flushed, worn face as he removed his cap, unbuttoned the top button of his tunic, and lit up a cancer stick. This cop is strictly Old School, and that's what we call him. He retires real soon and is taking it way easy til then. He has about as many tales to tell about "the way it used to be" as he has gray hairs on his head. Now he shook that big gray head and blew out Camel smoke.

"Benny the Booster is dead," he told us.

"No shit?"

"End of an era," mumbled Darrel Troy.

"Who's Benny the Booster?" asked a rookie, tolerated at the table because his dad and uncle were stand-up guys on the force, uptown.

"Who's Benny the Booster," Old School repeated,

blowing smoke and smirking at the rookie. Then he cocked his gray head at me: "*You* tell him."

I'd had a few encounters with Benny over the years, and for a character with a very forgettable face he was definitely unforgettable.

Talk about old-school characters! I scanned the rookie's fresh face and wondered if a kid like this, just out of the Academy, even knew the difference between a shoplifter and a booster, let alone the distinctions among boosters. Shoplifters weren't professionals, though they might be habituals. They were pilferers who stole compulsively or whimsically from stores. And low-level boosters, usually junkies or hookers, were just crude "clout and lam" (steal and split) thieves. But a world-class booster like Benny made it look easy, even magical — the kind of guy who could steal your socks without removing your shoes. He only got pinched by accident, or later by carelessness. You know how bicycle racers have to start out with certain God-given features — wiry, slim, not too tall or short — so too an ace booster is gifted with an anonymous look, like Benny: not tall or short, neither skinny nor fat, not cute, not ugly — and he hones his "gray man" persona as he learns his craft.

Benny was all craft. Started out selling stolen goods out of the trunk of a vintage Cad, venturing into hoods where even I wouldn't go without backup. Moved on up to running a private "store," a basement crib in a walkup on a shabby midtown block, where in-the-know buyers selected from his stockpile of high-end clothing and accessories. He was a loner, but gregarious enough to hit the bars and clubs where players, rounders, gangsters, and late-nite ladies congregated, and soon they were all his exclusive customers. The slickest pimps, call girls, and Mob guys in the city could afford to shop elsewhere, but they liked to buy hot "bargains" from Benny the Booster, the wised-up street guy who looked like a square from Delaware. His store was busted only once because he stayed too long in one location, and with all the felonious individuals coming and going it attracted attention. Shyster cronies helped him beat the rap, and they'd continue to keep Benny from doing time, for a hefty price.

He lived alone, out of hotel rooms. Traded his classy call-girl customers' expensive furs or gowns for no-nonsense sex. Drank moderately and abhorred drugs of any kind. And over the years he saved up quite a lot of cash, stashed in safe deposit boxes all over the city, cash which he was reluctant to spend, till, just when he was getting old, he got a little foolish in the heart department.

I didn't know him from Adam the first time I stumbled on Benny in action and muffed the collar. I was still a little green, hadn't been wearing the bag too long when I was detailed to surveil the main entrance of an upscale upper-eastside department store from behind a dirty second-floor office window across the avenue. The Desk had been tipped that a certain bigtime felon wanted on many counts was going to show at this posh store to buy his current honey a pricey gift. it was the honey who dropped the dime, because she said she was fed up with her rough, tough boyfriend's heavy-handed bullshit. Some honey. The tip might be nothing but hot air, so a House rookie, namely me, was sent over to scope the scene. If I got lucky, the Lieutenant said, I'd make a high-profile collar that would look great on my sheet. If not, well, it was all in a day's work.

I peered through that grime-stained window, looking down on all the people coming and going out of that big store, in and out, out and in. After a couple of hours I was bored out of my mind, but I still had to watch. The perp might be disguised, I was told, so I had to look sharp at all the humdrum civilians to see who matched the mug shots I'd been shown. And if I hadn't been looking real hard I'd never have noticed a regular-featured white male in a long loose coat who went in and came out maybe fifteen minutes later looking like he'd put on a lot of weight. I wasn't so green that I didn't make him for a booster. And I had a gut feeling (which was maybe only thirst or hunger) that the famous felon wasn't going to show, and even if he did show while I went down to check out this other guy, who really gave a shit? My tour was almost over, I could use a cool brew, and I wanted to move.

I ran down to the crowded avenue and spotted the 'fat' man in his big coat heading down into the Subway. I didn't want to shout "Halt!" and make a scene. Not yet. Maybe he'd paid for what he had on under his big coat. I had to get close enough to check him out and make the instant call of whether I should get in his face or not.

He was fast for a 'fat' guy. Too fast. As I skipped down the Subway steps, I saw him already passing through the turnstile as a just-arrived train opened its doors at the platform a few feet away from him. So I shouted out "Hey you! Stop! Police!" He heard me alright, but scuttled onto the train and the doors closed behind him. I ran back to the booth and called in the transit cops to board the train at the next stop. As luck and city budget cutbacks would have it, no transit cops were posted at the next station, but when two of them entered and swept the train at the next express stop, they found only a neat pile of sportscoats and slacks on an empty seat. The booster had jettisoned his swag when he saw them coming and had exited clean, undetectable, free.

I hadn't seen the perp's full face, but I got a good glance at his profile as he got on the Subway train. It was such an unremarkable profile that it stayed on my mind, and when I met him years later at his store bust, I recognized him immediately. But back when he gave me the slip in the Subway I shrugged off the incident. All in a day's work. If the job was about anything, I was learning, it was Expect the Unexpected.

"Ain't it the truth!" Old School guffawed. "But leave me interject my two-cents worth at this juncture, with all due respect, since I happen to go all the way back with Benny. We was in ninth grade together across the river, back when Middle School was still called Junior High. "Benny's folks were carny people, the Johnson family, drifting grifters whose traveling show folded. So his dad went to ballyhoo barking on the Coney Island boardwalk, and his mom ran a clip stand in the same amusement park. Benny appeared in our class one morning, the new kid on the block. He didn't look like a tough guy, but he didn't look like a wimp either. He didn't look like *any*thing. We couldn't peg him till he opened his mouth and started spouting doubletalk and carny slang. He didn't say much at first though, kinda quiet and shy, sussing out the situation. But that first day and often thereafter, when the kids got their paper-bag lunches out of the coat closet at lunchtime, more than one kid found his bag not as full as when he'd left home. Benny's folks didn't provide him with a bag lunch, you see. And he also was expected to hustle up his own spending money, which he sometimes did by selling us hot skin zones in the playground after lunch. 'You get the student discount because I got the five-finger discount,' he told me when I purchased a raunchy, split-beaver mag from him which you'd never see on our local newsstand racks. When he hustled those mags he sounded like a sideshow spieler, must have got it from his dad, and we knew he came from another, racier world we could only guess about.

"I was kind of a punk at the time, a wannabe hoodlum, and Benny sat next to me in the back of our class. We kind of became friends, or at least as friendly as Benny got with anyone. He even took me out to the Island one time to watch his dad — a deathly pale, skinny man with a pencil mustache — talk the suckers inside, and his mom, an aging floozy working a rigged ring-toss game. Business was slow, and she got us to shill for her: every few minutes, when there was a new crowd passing by on the boardwalk, we'd loudly jump for joy and yell that we'd won one of the unwinnable prizes, to bring the rubes over. She gave us a pack of Pall Malls for our time.

"Yeah, Benny already talked the talk and walked the walk. 'I don't have pretzel one today,' he'd say, 'so I guess I'll have to put the grab on some church poor boxes, or maybe roll a lush for chump change.' He talked like a little wiseguy but didn't look the part at all. He had a generic face, a nothing haircut, wore old clothes that didn't fit real good.

"Junior high graduation, we all had to rent those stupid dark robes and mortarboard caps with the tassel hanging down. Benny, who was absent a lot, always had a good excuse, and knew how to con the teacher with a poor-boy line. He told her his uncle was in the business and would rent the class its caps and gowns for half the price of the usual provider. How could she say no? So he brings in this big heap of caps and gowns and we all pay him with money from home. The teacher even praises him for his 'initiative.' I pay along with the others but I'm snickering 'cause I know Benny boosted all the graduation outfits from a big store downtown, a few at a time.

"My parents, like his, were both working — my folks ran

a laundry — and they didn't attend the stupid graduation ceremony on the sweltering football field at the end of June. After the ceremony, Benny collected all the caps and gowns like everything was on the up-and-up... and then he got me to help him carry and heave them into the dumpster behind the supermarket on the avenue, where he made sure they were stuffed down out of sight under a lot of garbage. Then he took me to the movies and bought me a milk shake and a burger after the show, maybe to buy my silence, but maybe not: he knew by then that I didn't feature snitches any more than he did.

"His folks moved on after the summer season, wherever, and he was gone with them, no goodbyes. Months later some kid who vaguely knew the Johnsons said Benny'd taken a fall and was off to Crime School (the reformatory), but I don't know about that. Next time I saw him was ten years later. I was a beat cop and he was driving by in a classic Coupe De Ville, didn't even see me. But some mope I was rousting said 'There goes Benny the Booster!' Anonymous looking, but he already had a name on the street.

"Yeah, Benny. I remember him back in Junior High with those caps and gowns. I knew he'd stolen them and I asked him how he did it. He gave me a sly smile and says 'I can't tell you that, but I can tell you one of my techniques: I wait around to go into a store until I see some hoody looking guy going in, or a bunch of teens, or even better, a colored guy or a Spic. The Security guys and the squares who run the store always keep their eyes on those types and I'm left alone to do my thing.' 'Wow, you're something else,' I told him. 'Yeah,' he smiled, 'but you're never as good as you wanna be, and you can always do better. Only suckers pat themselves on the back.' That was Benny, all of fifteen, looking like a no-style nebbish and a little too hip for his own good.

"Tell me about it," I said, recalling how overly courteous and even ingratiating Benny was when we took down his store. Of course the bust was just a blip on his screen. He had a tri-state itinerary so he never hit any one place too often, and he still worked solo all the time, never with a stall (diversionary accomplice) to throw a hump (create a distracting disturbance). He goes in, takes what he wants, and gets out, unobserved like he's invisible. If he ever gets busted, his shysters know how to get him out right away. Time goes by, he's getting up there, he still boosts Class-A stuff, takes orders from big-time baddies, stashes his cash, still gets his rocks off with hookers... until he meets up with Chlamydia Jane.

Jane (nee Jane Barlow, alias Jane Barnacle aka Jane Barney) was out there working one of her many scams at the time. Selling ads for non- existent periodicals by day, bamboozling rich old Cafe Society gents by night. Strictly a singleton like Benny, never married, never even anyone's mistress for long, she's her own woman all the way. She takes men for what they can give and then shines them on. And she's got the smarts and the classy bone structure to get away with it: looks like a retired runway model, grew up with money, paid her dues on the street. She can make it in any situation, and she does. If she's got a roguish stud for a boyfriend, she'll use him to play the badger game: Jane lures a well-off, very married mark to a specially prepared pad where he's secretly videoed getting down with her. Then the boyfriend busts in like an outraged husband or lover. Intimidation and/or blackmail squeezes big bucks from the vic, and Jane and her b.f. are gone with the wind.

Even after she got on the needle and her con game got sloppy, she could still pass for elegant and high-class. But when she took her shades off you saw the dead junkie eyes.

From cool, lucrative long-con scams she quickly descended to going on the buzz (purse snatching from moms pushing baby strollers) and soliciting contributions, dressed as a nun, for the "Orphanage for Wayward Girls." Then she started turning tricks to support her habit— she favored mainline shots of "whiz-bang," a deadly combo of coke and smack — and she was in and out of the Women's House of D (the grim downtown lockup), not bothering to fend off the bull dykes who ruled the roost and fought each other to claim her favors exclusively. I saw her being booked more than once and her attitude was fatalistically nonchalant: "You take a fall, you do the time."

Whenever she managed to get off the junk for a spell she had the chuck horrors (aversion to food) and had to take all kinds of pills so she wouldn't waste away. Then she'd always run into some addict she knew on the street, someone like Sam the Shmecker who had a manageable long-term habit and was making his bucks on the short con. Naturally she got back on the stuff.

Desperate for dope money again, she hung with some junkie thieves, the dregs of the underworld, particularly with a rough-trade biker and a sometime bodybuilder, two dudes who'd acquired serious joneses: they were cruise-boppers (fag rollers) who wanted to move on up to crib-cracking (burglary), and Jane was the getaway wheeler till they got nabbed. With another street weasel she blackmailed kiddie diddlers (pedophiles). Then, on her own again, she tried her hand at skin- clouting (boosting furs), which is when she met Benny the Booster.

Benny was casing this upscale emporium, setting up a score, when he sees this woman: she has a slim, haughty, voguey Euro look which spells Class to him. He watches her trying to walk out of the store wearing an expensive fur wrap like it's her own. No way is she going to make it past Security, Benny knows, with her blatant bluff. So he does something he's never done before: he plays the stall unasked, throwing himself down on the waxed floor, screaming and kicking and even foaming at the mouth.

Security guys and floorwalkers come a-running. And as he sees the voguey woman safely exiting with the boosted fur wrap on her back, he picks himself up and turns off the fit. "Sorry," he tells the store dicks. "I was just having a slight epileptic seizure." They nod coldly and eye him oddly as he hurries out of the store, blowing his own future score.

Benny catches up with Jane down the block, spells out why she was almost nabbed and why she wasn't, fills her in on some booster basics — and she's all ears. "Who is this old guy who looks like Mr. Nobody and raps like Daddy Cool?" she wonders.

They go for coffee. They're both in the life, they know what's what and who's who. They find they know some career criminals in common. They hit it off. She looks posh and hasn't got a dime, and he's still wearing old clothes but has heaps of cash stashed all over town. She's got a finely chiseled face with half-dead junkie eyes. He's got a knowing look on his Joe Blow mug. Currently he rents a single-occupancy unit with a hot plate in the Heartbreak Hotel. She's currently bedding down with one of the diesel dykes she met in detention, but the lezbo is too hot for hetero-type sex (i.e. dildo penetrations) and Jane is not turned on. Benny seems to know where she's at.

"Look," he tells her, "your tracks are showing, you got zombie eyes in a nice face, your whole vibe says Smack City and you know that loser powder is bad news, a one-way ticket to the bone orchard or the cackle factory. Am I right or am I right?"

"You're right on, but it's too hard to kick when you don't have much else to live for."

Then Jane pours out her heart to Benny like she never does to anyone, and he gets hung up on her like he never does on anyone. He takes her to a certain cabin colony Jerseyside where criminals go to chill in the country, and helps her to go cold turkey. They share a cabin, but no sex. Up front she says she has no eyes for sex with him or anyone else really, "So forget about balling me and we'll get along great." Benny says that's cool with him. He says he has a low-level libido easily satisfied by a professional once a month or so. "But you're my kind of woman," he tells her. Of course he has the quiet hots for her. Jane tells him "You look like an old dork but you're the coolest cat I know." They kind of team up, much as two loners can team up. All this I heard here and there, more or less, from people they knew on the street.

"So how *did* Benny buy it?" Darrel Troy asks Old School, who's stubbing out his smoke and rebuttoning his tunic. He has to get back to the Desk and put in an appearance before he goes home.

"I got no time," Old School sighs, checking his wristwatch.

"Hold your fricking horses," snorts Darrel. "Your whole fucking tour you either coop or lay dead, and *now* you're in a hurry? just tell us — how did Benny go?"

"Okay," said Old School, carefully placing his cap on his head just so. Then he turned to me. "Weren't *you* there at his final bust?"

I was. Benny and Jane didn't live together, but even though he was a cheapskate he spent some of his savings on her, bought her dope (she got back on the needle despite Benny's best efforts to help her kick) and paid the rent on a high-rise apartment where she could hole up solo and where he was always welcome. He spent a lot of time hanging with her, but still kept his room-and-a-half at the Heartbreak Hotel. When she wanted a suite of new furniture, he could easily have afforded buying her the best, but why spend when you could boost? That's how Benny's mind worked.

So Benny rents a uniform and a truck, pulls up at the warehouse of a big furniture outlet, produces a fake bill of lading, and gets two stock handlers to help him load up whatever — sofa, love seats, vanity — and rolls it all out on skids to the truck. This isn't his usual m.o, but he almost pulls it off, till a clear head up in the office makes a couple of calls and runs down to the loading dock shouting, "Stop that man!" The stock guys grab Benny, who's shy of being roughed up — he hates altercations, right? — so he throws up his hands and yells, "Call the cops!" They do, and I was working that tour when I got the call to pick him up.

Polite and cool, he came along to be booked without making any fuss. Now the shyster on retainer earned his keep. I had to show up three fricking times because his sleazeball lawyer kept asking for a continuance until the right judge was on the bench and the right prosecutor in court. Then all these worthies briefly conferred and Benny walked as a "first offender." His rap sheet had vanished from the files. On the way out he shook my hand. "Ain't it grand what money can do?" he said. I had to laugh. You couldn't get mad at Benny, you just couldn't.

"So what happened to him?" Darrel asked impatiently.

"Last night," Old School says, getting up to go, "Jane calls 911. Benny's had a heart attack at her place. He's DOA, and we bring her in for a statement. She's distraught, but she talks plenty. Says they had this real cool relationship, but after he got nabbed for trying to boost the furniture, now he said no matter what they'd agreed, he wanted to bone her, and she said she was like 'What the fuck, you wanna do me, go for it!' He did, and his heart burst just as he came in her. Then Jane mentioned she had the clap, probably in case anyone in the House had the idea of getting a free ride back in the blue room like in the old days. I offered her a lift to her apartment, which she'd have to give up now that Benny wouldn't be around to pay the fancy rent. She said she'd take the Subway on her own, thanks. I thought about Benny's hard-earned cash in all those metal boxes in banks around the city. He'd told her about his Safe Deposit savings, and she'd have to be thinking about that too. Well, she'd either clean up her act, get back on the con, maybe go down the junk toilet. What do I know? I couldn't tell her nothing but 'Good night and good luck!' And she came right back at me with 'It's not a good night, and I don't need your kind of luck, John Law!'"

"Good old Jane, a hard case to the end!" Troy said.

"I'm outta here," said Old School. On his way out of the diner he said something to the Turk and the Turk laughed heartily.

We sat there for a while, not saying much, DDT and me and a couple of other badge-men who'd come in as we were talking about Benny the Booster and Chlamydia Jane (DDT had dubbed her that when she infected a badge years ago). The rookie had gone back to the House in the middle of the story; he couldn't care less about any characters from the dinosaur days, no matter how colorful, you could tell by his bored, deadpan expression.

"I wonder why Jane didn't throw old Benny a hump before last night," Darrel asked no one in particular. "She'd done just about everyone else in town."

“Because she really liked him,” I said quietly. Darrel spritzed his lips at that, flapping his hand at me like shooing away a fly. “Go figure women,” I added.

“Go figure anybody!” Darrel capped me. Then we had to go. Coffee break was over. From behind the register, the Turk rang up “No Sale” and waved us out with a smile.

We walked up the sooty sidewalk to the House, not saying anything. Just another day on the mean streets of the naked city. Benny the Booster was dead, we were still alive, and Jane was, too, if junkies can be said to be truly alive. But DDT can turn anything into a joke. Now whenever he hears anyone say, “Good luck!” he'll pipe up, loud and clear: “I don't need your kind of luck, John Law!”

About the Author

Jon Horn's writing has appeared in the *New York Times Sunday Travel Section, Honeysuckle, Gallery, Crawdaddy,* the recently published Brit anthology, *Infernal Mysteries,* the *New Olympia Reader,* and even more obscure venues. “Benny the Booster & Chlamydia Jane“ is from Jon Horn's as-yet-unpublished *Perp Street* about NYC cops on and off-duty and other law breakers. He's lived or traveled on four continents and currently resides with his family in the state his license plate says is the Land of Enchantment.

BLOOD IS BLOOD

SEAN JACQUES

BOREDOM BLEW through Bo's lips as his fingers tapped the steering wheel.

He glimpsed the clock on the dash.

1:17 p.m.

Goddamn. Just how late was she going to be?

Parked in his Ford pickup at Dutch's roadside gas station, he fell back to watching cars and trucks infrequently pass by on the two-lane highway. Not much call for gas today. And with it being the second Saturday in November, not many were looking to rent a canoe or buy a pound of fishing worms that Dutch's offered as a summer specialty.

It was two nights ago when his older sister, Debbie, had called him. Out-of-the-blue. They'd not seen each other since their father's funeral six years back. Before then, it was a couple years earlier at their mom's. It was odd enough just to hear from Debbie, but she seemed scattered-brained. Angry. A little scared. The only sense he could decipher out of her cryptic jabbering was that she wanted him to take care of her 15-year-old son. Some sort of trouble had exploded. Bo didn't ask why she had called him for such a favor, but the question had been lingering in his mind. There'd never been what you might call a sibling bond between them, she'd been calling him a no-account most of his life, so it was hard to believe that she was now begging for his no-account ass to be the landing spot to dump off her own brood.

The blinker of a red Lexus started flashing and when it turned into Dutch's lot, Bo saw a face behind the windshield that was not unlike his own. He tooted the horn and raised his arm out the truck window and the car angled toward him.

They stepped out at the same time, exchanging awkward "heys," and met in an awkward hug. She signaled for her passenger son to wait inside the car, and when she looked back at Bo, tears were welling in her eyes.

"Can we talk?" she whispered.

He nodded and she went around to the other side of his pickup and let herself in while he got back in the driver's seat. Letting her find her bearings, he glimpsed through the window of the Lexus and noticed the kid's mop of unkempt wavy purple hair.

"I don't know what to do with him," she said. "He's too much."

"Too much of what?"

"Too much for me." The tears dropped and her hands went to shaking. "He keeps getting into fights at school and arguing with his teachers. He got suspended again last week and I doubt if they'll let him back in. I can hardly get him out of his room while he's home, all he does is sit on that damn phone all day and yells if I even try to make him do anything." She rubbed the back of her hand across her wet cheek. "And this latest thing... "

Bo held his eyes on her, waiting for it.

"He set the neighbor's fence on fire."

"On purpose?"

"He says he was only playing around, but they're threatening to press charges. And expecting me to pay an arm and leg for a new fence."

"How much you need?"

She shot him a dirty look.

"I'm not asking for your money, Bo."

He bowed his head, knowing she took offense.

"What about your ex?"

"Derrick?" She snorted. "He's too busy raising his two other little shits with that ugly Asian bitch he's married to now."

"Well, what exactly do you want from me?"

"I need a break." She wiped her eyes.

"How long a one?"

She couldn't answer. But her face pleaded.

Bo turned and studied the kid again then he looked back at her with a wry grin. "He's not gonna burn me out is he?"

"It's not fucking funny, Bo," she snapped. "This is serious."

"It's a serious question."

He rolled his lips together, considering the answer he would give her. Long ago, he'd started abiding by a code that said never cause shit for others and don't bring somebody's shit on yourself. But in this case, blood is blood.

"Why me?"

She heaved. "Because you're the only person I know who could take care of it."

"It?"

He gave her a puzzled glance.

Dutch's was the midway point between Debbie's three-story outside KC and Bo's double-wide in the Ozarks, and the hilly route back to his place took roughly two-and-half hours. The kid kept to whatever it was he was doing on his iPhone, and anytime Bo asked him if the radio music was too loud or if it was warm enough in the cab, the only reply was "Doesn't matter," so Bo didn't encourage a conversation.

About halfway through the drive, the kid's phone ran out of juice, so he leaned his head against the door glass and shut his eyes. Bo glimpsed at his weirdo nephew every now and again, studying the pale, pimply face, purple hair, and scrawny frame. He wondered how Debbie could've sprung such defective offspring. She was supposed to be the alpha, the one who amounted to something. Finance degree at Mizzou. Wife of a slick-talking corporate lawyer. Sunday school teacher. All this time, he'd figured she'd reached the pinnacle of whatever she wanted out of her perfect life, but now it appeared that all she'd earned from her efforts was a bitter divorce from a two-timing cheat and a nutty son and a whole lot of self-loathing. Funny how fate works out when the family ledger is tallied.

By the time the November sun was tingling the tops of the Ozark hills, they had killed the state highway part of the trip. The kid had been asleep for the past hour, missing the series of curvy county roads, but as the pickup turned onto gravel, he startled awake with a slight fright when seeing the closed-in maze of winter-bare trees.

"Where are we?"

"About there."

"Isn't there a town?"

"Closest one was twenty miles back."

The kid swallowed and stared out the windshield with fright on his face.

"Where are you taking me?"

Bo tossed him a sideways glance. "Home."

After another series of winding bends the gravel turned to dirt and they came upon a Chevy truck on the side of the road. On the open tailgate sat an elderly couple dressed in camouflage and blaze orange, and in the bed lay a bloody, gutted deer.

Bo slowed and rolled down his window as he pulled up next to them and stopped.

"What'd you get, Nate?" he asked the grizzled-looking man.

"I didn't get jackshit. But this little spike buck accidentally wandered right up into Mary's sights."

"We's walkin' back from our stands and there he stood not twenty feet from this road," Mary piped up. "Could've saved ourselves a long day perched up in a tree."

"Reckon he was tryin' to steal your truck?"

"He mightta been. How 'bout you, you get your monster this mornin'?"

Bo shook his head. "Naw, I didn't make it out today." He nudged his chin toward the kid. "This is my sister's boy. Kevin. He's gonna be stayin' with me this week."

"Bringin' him huntin'?" Mary inquired.

Bo glanced at the kid and frowned. "No, I doubt that."

Kevin looked blankly at Bo then put his head down.

"Come on by the house if you like," Mary offered, "and I'll set you up with some backstrap for supper."

"Well, appreciate the offer. But I best get us settled in tonight. Maybe later on in the week." He shifted his pickup into gear. "Ya'll be good."

"Take care, now," Ed said with a smile and wave. "Good luck gettin' your monster."

As they drove away from the kind killers, Kevin craned his head around to continue watching them. “They shot it?”

“She did, sounds like.”

“Why?”

“They’s huntin’.”

Kevin kept his stare on them until their shapes disappeared behind the dark trees.

After another mile, Bo turned onto a two-path dirt driveway and crawled toward a two-acre clearing where sat a double-wide trailer with a wooden porch deck. A rusty ’70 Mustang Cobra raised up on cinder blocks was parked in the front yard, and on the far side of the clearing was a hundred or so cut logs of assorted sizes lying in disorder. Besides the three ricks of piled firewood, some of the logs had been carved into standing statues of bears and owls and crows and the like. Behind the trailer stood a tool shed, a garage barn, a smokehouse, and a chicken pen with ten squawking hens inside it. At the edge of the yard, a stack of hay bales had a bullseye target stabbed in its center.

As the pickup came closer, a border collie and blue-eyed hound came running toward them, barking and wagging tails. Bo parked and cut the engine next to the Mustang. “Don’t mind the dogs,” he told the kid. “They jus’ beg for attention is all.”

He stepped out and rolled his hands over their muzzles then grabbed the kid’s suitcase out of the truck bed and headed toward the porch. Kevin remained in the cab, digesting the lonesome place, then he slid out of the passenger side and hightailed to the front door for fear of being left alone.

When they stepped inside the temperature was cool, so Bo went to tossing firewood into the iron woodstove to spark up some warmth. The kid eyed the deer antlers on the walls, plus the turkey feather art pieces in glass frames. There were also dozens of wood-carved animals, some a foot tall, others the size of a pea, lounging around the living room, and mounted over the television were two beautifully designed recurve bows with beaded leather quivers and a stretched-out coyote hide.

"Spare bed's on the left." Bo pointed. "The bathroom is the first door on the right. You're welcome to anything in the fridge, except the beer."

"Where do I charge my phone?"

"There's an outlet right over there on the wall. Or there's one in your room."

"Is there a password for wi-fi?"

"A what?"

"I need to connect to wi-fi, is there a password?"

Bo chuckled. "No, I don't have wi-fi."

"How do you connect to the internet then?"

"Don't have that either."

Kevin's face dropped like he'd just learned that his pet hamster died.

"I got a DVD player and a box of movies I picked up at a yard sale. A few old westerns and crime flicks, and I think there's some funny ones in there."

Kevin started for the spare bedroom and disappeared into it without another word.

"You want some hotdogs?" Bo called out. "All I gotta do is heat 'em on the stove." When no response came back, Bo shook his head. "Squirrelly son of a gun."

The next morning, Bo was up at six. He made eggs and bacon and coffee and ate it all while looking out the back window and meditating on what he might do on this Sunday. The temperature wasn't expected to rise above 45°.

He thought about whittling some stick figures. The trinket seller from Branson had called him this week, saying he needed inventory for Christmas. Maybe the kid could find interest in helping. Hard to tell. Then he started to wonder what the hell he was going to do with the kid when he went to work tomorrow. Leaving him here, by himself, might not be such a good idea. The guns were locked away, but there were axes and knives and sharp tools lying around. And full cans of gas. He then decided that tomorrow was tomorrow, he could figure out this dilemma later, and he headed outside to do some damage to today.

It wasn't until eleven that the kid woke up and stumbled outside, looking like a vampire in need of a transfusion. Like the submissive dogs lying on the ground, he plopped down next to them and watched his chainsaw-carving uncle cut claws into the paws of an eight-foot-tall standing bear. Bo shut off the chainsaw. He pulled off his googles and shook sawdust out of his woolly hair and flicked off some more from his shirt with his hands.

"Not much of a rise-and-shine, are you?"

The kid glanced up at him, then pulled his chin back down as quick as he'd risen it.

"You hungry?"

"Doesn't matter."

"Doesn't matter." Bo smirked.

They headed back inside the trailer and Bo found some smoked ham to make sandwiches. They settled down at the small dining table to feast, and between his nibbling, the kid kept pecking his phone, grumbling about the weak cell service.

"How do you not have wi-fi or internet?"

"Don't have a need for it."

"How do you know what's going on?"

"I look out the window." Bo rubbed his whiskered chin. "From what I can tell, all those phones do is clutter your brain and drop you down into a rabbit hole of thinkin' about things that really ain't worth thinkin' about to start with. That, and sharin' pictures of yourself showin' how great your life is, when it ain't."

The kid bit into his sandwich and chewed. Washed it down with a can of Dr. Pepper. "So all you do is make this stuff?" he asked, eyeing the carvings in the room.

"No, I haul for a livin'. That takes up most of my week. I jus' carve for somethin' to do in my spare time."

"Don't you do anything fun?"

"I hunt. Fish when I can." Bo crushed his soda can. "Go to Springfield once or twice a month. Usually check out Bass Pro and a restaurant or movie if I go with a lady friend."

"Like a girlfriend?"

"Somethin' like that, yeah." Bo smiled. "You like girls?"

The kid went back to pecking his fingers on his phone. Bo shook his head over the kid's peculiarity. He rose from the table and got a Budweiser out of the fridge. He cracked it open and angled across the living room to look out the front window. He didn't care to carve more logs today. Neither did he desire to ticker on the Mustang. What he really wished for was to be out in the hollers with his thirty-ought, tracking a buck, like he had intended to do today before this alien dropped in his lap. Or maybe spending the rest of the day rolling in the sack with one of his go-to women who would happily speed out here to see him if only he called.

He turned around to see the kid still stationed at the kitchen table, doing only god knows what on that damn phone. He couldn't picture the kid gathering enough gumption to try such a stunt as burning down a neighbor's fence, but still, he didn't know what the kid was capable of.

"So tomorrow," he started in. "You think you'll be alright out here by yourself?"

Kevin threw his attention up.

"What?"

"I go to work around six. I gotta trust you not to get into anything you shouldn't."

"I'm not staying here by myself."

"Well, yeah, you're gonna have to."

"Fuck you!" Kevin erupted from the table. "Fuck you!!"

Bo squeezed his brows tight, surprised by the kid's heated reaction.

"What's the problem here, bud?"

"Take me back home!"

Bo stared at the kid, baffled. "I jus' made a five-hour roundtrip to get you yesterday, I'm not gonna turn around today and do it all over again—"

"—She only wants to get rid of me!"

Bo chomped his teeth, his jaws pulsating, his body growing stiff.

"You can't leave me here!" Kevin yelled, his cheeks blooming red.

"Why? You scared or somethin'?"

"You can't leave me here!"

Bo could sense the terror within the kid, like watching a rabbit hooked on barb wire.

"You can't leave me here! You can't leave me here!"

Kevin collapsed into a heap of whimpering.

Bo stood still, now understanding what his sister meant by not knowing what to do with him. "I'm not wantin' to get rid of you," he lied, trying to calm the kid. "But my boss counts on me to haul logs from the woods to the mill, cause if I don't, then there's no work for the guys at the mill, and if there's no work, ain't nobody makes their livin' tomorrow."

"Then take me with you," Kevin bawled.

"I can't be havin' you in the log truck with me—"

"—Why not?"

"Cause I can't have anybody with me—"

"—Fuck you!"

"Hey!" Bo raised his voice. "Watch your mouth!"

"I know you don't want me here! You hate me! Everyone hates me!"

"I brought you here with me, didn't I? I'd say that's a far cry from hate."

"Fuck you! Fuck you!" The kid fell into despondent blubbering.

Bo bowed his head in restraint and blew his chagrin out his lips. "Yeah... fuck me high and hard." Then he set his beer on the window seal and walked out the front door for a breath of country air.

Bo shared a cold silence with the kid for the rest of the afternoon. No use spilling more rotten apples out of the broken bucket. At five, he grudgingly called his boss, Dubb Boetticher, with word that he wouldn't be able to make it into work tomorrow. Family problems, he'd rather not get into details. Boetticher, a well-off sawmiller who also rented out Bo's double-wide and owned the 1,200 acres of wilderness surrounding it, pushed him on how much time he needed, but Bo couldn't answer, he just kept apologizing for letting the mill down. Boetticher told him not to be so hard on himself, hell, he'd not skipped a day of work in two years. Bo listened but couldn't shake his guilt. Whenever he gave his word to do something, he meant it, and he couldn't buck the feeling that he was welching on one of the few people he'd given his word to.

For the rest of the evening, he and the kid shared a silent supper of fried potatoes and fried chicken, followed by a viewing of Wyatt Earp bringing hell with him on TV. The kid then wandered off to bed at nine. Bo went at ten, but sleep was not sound. Too much pondering over what to do with the kid. Too much disappointment in Debbie for raising what appeared to be a dead end for the family legacy. To believe that their good old mom and dad used to pester him that he should be more like his smart and pretty big sister, that he should apply himself toward some meaning in the world, go back to high school and get a diploma, stop fooling around with fast cars and quick girls and dangerous drink, go do something rewarding for himself. Well, turns out, looks like he's the chosen cherry to carry out the family legacy now.

The third day. Bo got up at six, even though he wasn't going to work. He poured a fresh cup of coffee and squinted out the window at the sunlight glowing blue in the dying darkness. He wished he was out there hunting. But as it stood, it looked like the kid was winning the war of wills. He wallowed in his defeat a bit longer, then tired of it, he decided it was time to take care of this once and for all.

He marched to the spare bedroom door, swung it open, and flipped on the light switch. “Get your ass up, and if you want to squabble about it, then I’ll leave you here all goddamn day!” Then he slammed the door back shut.

After a rebellious twenty minutes, the kid ambled out, rubbing his eyes, his face marbled sullen. Bo sat at the kitchen table, finishing off what was left in his coffee mug.

“I’m stayin’ home from work,” Bo announced in a tone that hinted that he did not wish to be fucked with any longer. “I’m not expectin’ a thank you, but you might do somethin’ besides makin’ me watch you finger that goddamn phone all day.”

“Like what?”

Bo exhaled hard through his nose.

“How ‘bout we take the Polaris out?”

“What’s that?”

“My four-wheeler. Take a ride through the woods.”

“Why?”

“You ever been in the woods?”

Kevin looked down at the table. “No.”

Bo swirled the feeble remains of cold coffee at the bottom of his cup.

“Go get yourself dressed. I’ll fix you some eggs and bacon.”

“Ok.”

“Ok?”

“I said, ok.”

The kid stood and wandered back to the spare bedroom.

While Kevin took his time nibbling his breakfast, Bo tossed on a blaze-orange vest and cap and grabbed his thirty-ought, then went outside to the shed to fire up the Polaris. He locked the rifle onto the gunrack and pulled the muddy 4x4 out into the yard and patiently waited for the kid, rubbing the fur of his roused dogs.

Kevin's face was bone pale when he walked out the back door. He slow-walked to the Polaris and, as he crouched into the passenger side, he noticed a spare blaze-orange coat and the racked rifle. What's this for?"

"For you." He revved the engine. "Get in and buckle up. Gets a little bouncy."

Kevin warily hopped aboard and off they rode, Bo yelling back at the dogs to stay home.

With the engine sputtering and the tires crushing dead leaves, they wound their way through miles of winter gray timber, rolling over hills, curling around logs, twisting around stumps, Kevin's knuckles squeezed white onto the rollbar, Bo jostling in the captain's chair. Every so often, Bo would comment on sculpted rock formations carved out over the centuries, or would name each chickadee, red-bellied woodpecker, and dark-eyed junco darting through the branches, or the red-tailed hawks circling above their heads. He stopped and showed the kid the fresh droppings where gobblers and hens had scratched that morning, and then, when they startled up three leaping deer and watched their flapping white tails disappear down into a holler, Bo steered the Polaris beneath a deer stand built twenty feet up a tree.

"I built that one four years back," Bo said, his breath blowing white fog from the cold. "I've taken three bucks with my bow out of it before, but I ain't seen anything but those same does this fall."

"You shoot them from up there?"

"Yep. Lot of waitin' to get a decent shot."

"Doesn't seem fair."

"Well neither is their sense of smell and how fast they can skedaddle."

Bo cut the engine and unbuckled his seat belt.

"Put that coat on. Let's take us a little walk."

"Why?"

"Jus' come on."

They got out of the Polaris and Kevin followed his uncle's swishing steps across the forest floor, blowing warmth into his cold hands. Crows cawed from the wintery sky. Squirrels scurried among the dead leaves. A few hundred yards from the deer stand, Bo halted then moved toward an oak where the leaves and dirt had been scraped away at its base.

"See here?" Bo said, pointing down. "Hoof prints."

Kevin strode closer and bent down for a gander.

"Probably been here less than an hour ago," Bo added.

A faraway gunshot went off.

Kevin jumped back, his eyes wide and whirling.

Bo turned his head in the direction of the boom. "Somebody mightta jus' got themselves somethin'." Then a second and third shot rang out. "Or maybe not." He ran his fingers over the hoof prints. "Young buck. Have to save him for my bow. I only gun-shoot monsters."

"Monsters?" the kid said softly.

"That's what I call an old buck with a monster rack on him. There's one I seen, I counted fourteen points on him this year, hooves are damn near as big as your fist. But he keeps to himself in the thickets and brush about three or four ridges over that way, won't let himself be open enough to get shot." Bo squinted toward the ridges. "He knows what he's doin'."

"You're hunting him because of his antlers?"

Bo chuckled at the kid.

"No. I'm not huntin' him for his antlers. I'm wantin' to honor who he is."

"By killing it?"

Bo was beginning to believe the kid might be genuinely affected by these woods, but then he remembered how the kid could turn on a dime, withdraw, or unleash. His mind then fell back to the monster and the kid's question. Though he didn't say it, deep down, he knew that he would not pull the trigger if he ever found the monster in his gunsight. The monster was beyond death, a mortal creature that had carved out its own holy existence in this age-old sanctuary, and Bo knew that he didn't possess enough heart to kill it simply because he could. "All right then, let's get back to the Polaris and see what else we might see."

Bo turned and headed the other way with the mopey kid following. Before they reached the Polaris, the noise of rustling leaves halted them. There stood a deer forty yards away, appearing as if it'd blossomed out of the wind. A gaunt six-pointer. Ribs and hips poking through its matted tan coat. It tottered on wobbly legs before falling forward.

"Something's wrong with it," Bo said in a low tone. "Probably Chronic Waste Disease. Makes 'em goofy and not act right."

The buck managed to lift its backside by its hind legs, but struggled to fully raise itself up onto its forelegs in front. It was like witnessing a zombie dig out of a grave. Bo couldn't help but compare it to his pathetic nephew.

Bo strode to the Polaris, keeping his sight on the ghostly buck, and freed the thirty-ought from the rack. Then he pulled the bolt up and back to shove a round into the chamber.

"What are you going to do?" the kid wondered.

Bo didn't answer as they both studied the shaky-standing buck. Its ears drooping, tongue wagging. Then fighting his better judgment, Bo told himself that a mercy killing is what the kid really needed, and what better moment than now.

"You gonna do it?" He glanced at the kid. "Or me?"

"Do what?"

Bo ignored the touch of horror crackling within the kid's voice and lifted the thirty-ought up so the kid could see. "The safety is right here. You push it to the other side and it's off, see the red? You keep this safety on 'til you're ready pull the trigger. That's rule one."

He stretched the rifle out for the kid to take it.

"What do you want me to do?" the kid mumbled.

"Take it."

The kid was getting more scared.

"I said, take it."

The kid reluctantly accepted the gun from his woodsman uncle and cradled it to his bony chest. Bo stepped behind him and squared his shoulders. He could feel the kid's arms shaking.

"Okay, bring the front around and peek through the scope with your eye."

The kid stretched the barrel straight and peeped through the scope.

"You see that thin cross?"

The kid nervously nodded his head.

"Now put the middle of that cross right on his midsection. Then move it up slowly toward his neck and hold it there."

Bo let go, allowing the kid to get a feel for the aim.

"When you think you got it, push the safety off, then

move your finger, real soft like, on the trigger. Don't squeeze or jerk it yet though, jus' see the shot first."

Kevin lowered the gun, shook his head.

"I can't do it."

"You can't? Or you don't want to?"

The kid shook his head again. Sniffled. Kept stone still, staring at the ground.

Bo wasn't used to seeing people cry, but this was the third time in three days he'd seen damp cheeks, once from his sister, twice from the kid, and it was making him damn uncomfortable and pissed and disappointed. He glanced to notice the disoriented buck wandering further away with its weaving steps.

"Hand me back my gun and I'll show you—"

The thirty-ought boomed and Bo dropped dead like a sack of cornmeal.

About the Author

Sean Jacques was raised in the Missouri Ozarks and now resides in southern California. His debut novel, *Doe Run*, is available from Shotgun Honey Books, and his short stories, plays, and poems can be found in several crime and grit lit publications, including *Starlite Pulp Review, Cowboy Jamboree, Punk Noir, Pulp Modern,* and *Reckon Review.* Find out more about him and his literary works @ seanjacque-sauthor.com.

THE WISHES OF THE BISHOP

ROBERT SLENTZ-KESLER

THE SEX PARTIES at Crackerbox Mansion were legendary.

In those days long ago in 1979, when the quiet town of Paxton in Northern Virginia still had only 8,000 people, and its bucolic charm, and its long roads through farm fields were not yet overrun by BMW-driving commuters from Washington DC, and the people there did not yet exercise or drink filtered water, and the narrow downtown streets were not yet jammed with bars and brewpubs and coffee shops and clean, pretty mothers in Volvo station wagons, there was a large, old four-square house on Cornwall Street that the local hippies called Crackerbox Mansion.

Crackerbox Mansion! Four young nurses from Rockland County Hospital shared the house — dubbed by Nurse Elaine after the Josie Brown song. Within a week of finalizing their rental agreement, they started hosting the town's wildest parties, and then one day while shopping in Arlington, Nurse Pamela happened on the going-out-of-business sale of a church supply store. She returned to the house with a car full of gear: clergy tunics and stoles and hats, icons of Mary and Jesus, all sizes of crucifixes and scepters, paintings of saints and apostles, incense burners and candle snuffers. So the Four Nurses decided that the sex parties at Crackerbox Mansion would henceforth have religious themes, with strict rules and rituals, and that interactions among partyers would follow liturgical protocol.

"Schlitz be with you."

"And also with you."

And so on.

Oh, the joy of Crackerbox Mansion, with its copious quantities of marijuana — the joints, the doobies, the fatties — and the endless flow of beer. It was like fresh air to the young people in that stagnant, lifeless town. Crackerbox Mansion allowed you to drop your facade, to enter and rejoice in who you were and who you wanted to become, even if only for one night.

Late every Friday afternoon as dusk descended gently on the town, Josh the Bosh would rev up his Harley Davidson XLH Sportster in the yard, then ride up the porch steps and through the front doorway into the house and tear through all four rooms on the bottom floor, yelling and whooping past the others who raised their beer cans as his flapping beard whizzed by. He would exit back down the front steps into the yard, kick out the stand to park his bike, and hold his arms up wide to address the throng gathered on the porch.

"Crackerbox Mansion Welcomes You!"

"Thanks Be To Josh!"

And so the weekend began.

Way on the other side of town on Monroe Street, just over the abandoned Washington & Old Dominion rail line, lived the very proper and upstanding Richard Prichard with his wholesome wife and their perfect children. Mr. Prichard wanted nothing more than to manage his respectable family in the traditional town of Paxton and to keep the culture of Paxton close to its colonial roots. That house of iniquity on Cornwall Street was a scandal, a blight on their beautiful village. Many local citizens joined Richard Prichard in loudly and publicly condemning the Four Nurses and their mansion of shame, but then on weekends some of those same citizens could be found partaking inside Crackerbox Mansion — getting it on, as it were — before sneaking back by daybreak to their quiet and virtuous lives.

Mr. Prichard's two children were impeccable and his wife Mrs. Prichard was clean and pretty (and because she was ahead of her time, drove, you guessed it, a Volvo station wagon). Even those children were heard quoting Words of Consecration from the Crackerbox Mansion liturgy — "Schlitz be with you!" — while holding up small cartons of chocolate milk in the lunchroom at Catoctin Elementary School. Mr. Prichard was outraged that his own children knew these words, that the wickedness of that house was seeping out into the community. Crackerbox Mansion must be destroyed, burned to the ground, and those nurses, those Jezebels, must be run out of town.

But the partying people of Crackerbox Mansion pressed forward, full steam ahead, and they just laughed at Richard Prichard and called him Dick Prichard and hung a small naked mannequin of him on a wall next to the painting of Saint Philip, and when someone sewed on a tiny fabric penis, it was only natural ever after that the mannequin was referred to as Little Richard. Partyers walking past that wall would ask for a blessing from Saint Philip and then flick the fabric penis of Little Richard Prichard. Such were the rituals of Crackerbox Mansion.

And from these rituals grew more intricate ceremonies in various rooms of that house, until games were conceived and developed, all with their own liturgies: The Confessional, Venereal Vespers, The Fourteen Stations of the Crotch, and The Wishes of the Bishop.

The Wishes of the Bishop! Among the collection of church gear was a bishop's hat, an absurdly tall miter with two high pointy rising peaks and sides that puffed out and two fringed flaps that hung down the back. Its cloth was originally plain linen, but as with all the religious icons and ornaments and sartorial accoutrements in Crackerbox Mansion, Theresa, Connie, Pamela, and Elaine sat at the kitchen table with their sewing kits decorating and denigrating the sacred miter, and soon the bishop's hat was adorned with embroidered breasts and penises and smiley faces with tongues out. Nurse Pamela disappeared into the storage closet and emerged with a six-foot long solid oak staff, an electric drill, a 1/4-inch drill bit, a sturdy double-sided screw, and a ten-inch rubber phallus. After fifteen minutes of careful work, she had affixed the schlong to the top of the staff, and so was born the Holy Dildo Scepter to accompany the hat. And then after another hour of sipping Chartreuse and brainstorming and sketching and drafting and writing, the nurses had created this new game — The Wishes of the Bishop.

These were the rules of The Wishes of the Bishop:

1. Whoever dons the bishop hat shall remain the Bishop for the duration of the game.
2. The duration of the game shall be thirty minutes.

3. Along with the Bishop, there may be up to three acolytes who participate in the game.
4. Acolytes shall self-identify by donning vestments — purple tunics that shall hang on the front hall coat rack.
5. Acolytes shall participate in the liturgy with fervent devotion and with full subservience to the Bishop.
6. Throughout the liturgy, participants shall employ the Exchange of Consent, which exchange shall be directed by the Bishop.

And so the game often began thus:

Bishop: "The Bishop wishes for you to follow her upstairs."

Acolyte(s): "I submit to the wishes of the Bishop."

"The Bishop wishes for you to remove your clothes."

"I submit to the wishes of the Bishop."

"The Bishop wishes for you to slowly unzip her leather boots."

And so on.

While anyone was welcome to take up the Bishop's miter and Holy Dildo Scepter, priority was bestowed upon the Four Nurses. When the Bishop was seen reverently strolling around the party with the scepter in one hand and a drink in the other, stopping to visit and chat with groups of guests, any partygoer wishing to participate in the game could go to the coat rack in the front hall and select a purple tunic. Once all vestments were in place, the Bishop would approach the first participant and begin the liturgy with the Exchange of Consent before processing up the back staircase with her entourage.

The game caught on like wildfire. Attendance at

Crackerbox Mansion skyrocketed, both for the games on the weekends as well as the impromptu — à-la-carte as it were — activities all over the furniture and floors and tables and even the washing machine and dryer in the kitchen. On occasion, someone with poor judgment would go a bit too far (overly ambitious insertion of various eucharistic utensils, for example), and one of the nurses would grab a nearby first aid kit and take care of things. Their commitment to safety and their ability to handle minor crises inhouse went a long way toward insulating Crackerbox Mansion from the townspeople of Paxton, but the catchy and addictive liturgy quotes continued to leak out into the broader community, especially among schoolchildren.

"The Bishop wishes for you to give back her glue stick right now!"

"No. I do *not* submit to your wishes. I had it first."

"Give it back or I'll flick your penis!"

Richard Prichard was at the boiling point. The increasingly wider reach of these liturgy lines further convinced him that this wasn't simply an issue of allowing people to do what they wanted to do inside the privacy of their own homes — no, the wickedness was spilling out and poisoning the youth of Paxton. Mr. Prichard had always suspected that these liberal bohemians wanted to corrupt young people and this proved it — they were coming for our children.

But as always, the Nurses ignored the outside world and continued their work of improving the sex games at Crackerbox Mansion. Lately, there had been complaints about the length of time for the Bishop game, that thirty minutes was far too short because things only started to get really interesting around that time. And so the Nurses convened a synod at the kitchen table and made it official:

the new time allotment for The Wishes of the Bishop would henceforth be a full two hours.

It was a Friday evening in early October when the new two-hour rule for The Wishes of the Bishop was instituted. The party was underway, drinks were poured, joints were lit, and Nurse Pamela who was in charge of the stereo system loaded the TEAC machine with the Friday reel of music: Cheap Trick, Bad Company, The Eagles, Fleetwood Mac, and dozens of other carefully curated selections.

"The Bishop game, it's two hours now, can you believe it?"

"That's too long, man, too damn long."

"I dare you to put on a tunic tonight."

"Not me, man, no way."

The evening progressed, smoke and music filled every room, people coupled or tripled on the couches in the front parlor or on the plush carpet in the back room. The three purple tunics hung on the coat rack by the door for a long time, no one would touch them. But then an hour later after dark descended and the lights dimmed, the tunics had disappeared, all three of them.

"Where did they go?"

"Who are the acolytes?"

"Over there."

Three young men stood quietly together by the kitchen door sipping cans of Schlitz. No one had seen them before, and no one knew — certainly not the three themselves — that they were about to become part of Crackerbox Mansion mythology. On this momentous night, they were the avant-garde of a new era.

Josh the Bosh walked over to them. "Hey, you guys know about those tunics, right?"

"Yeah, we've heard about the Bishop. We're ready, man!"

"Yeah, we know all about it. I submit to the wi —"

"Stop!" said Josh. "You say the words only at the appropriate time."

"Right, man, right. Sorry."

"And it's two hours now," said Josh. "You know that right?"

"Oh, we heard it was thirty minutes."

"New rule starting tonight, just thought you should know."

"She descends!"

Nurse Theresa appeared on the back staircase wearing the Bishop's hat and gripping the Holy Dildo Scepter. She wore a short black robe hemmed with sequins just above her knees, and a side slit that rose up to the top of her thigh. Her long block-heel purple leather boots hugged tight to her calves and knees.

"Oh god, it's her," said one of the boys.

"Wow, look at her."

"We're in, man! I can't wait."

Josh raised his beer can to them and said, "Alright, you guys are on your own."

Theresa stepped off the final stair and walked through the dining room. With her boot heels and the high miter Bishop's hat, she towered over everyone. She greeted partyers with smiles and nods, holding a martini glass in her right hand and the scepter in her left. She walked through every room to greet her guests, even those already disrobed and enmeshed in activities of their own. And finally, she approached the three boys by the kitchen door and stood before them.

Someone turned the music down. All talking stopped. The boys stood wide-eyed.

"Uh, hello, we're —"

"Shut up dude, I don't think we're supposed to talk."

Theresa stood silent. She extended her martini glass off to her side and someone took it from her, then she reached out and ran a finger along the shoulder of the boy nearest her. She touched his face, his cheek, his chin. She gazed at the other two. And then she spoke.

"You'll do." She grinned and nodded. "You'll do quite nicely."

The boys said nothing.

"The Bishop wishes for all three of you to follow her to The Office. Now." She turned away and strode to the stairs.

They stumbled after her. "We submit to the wishes of the Bishop!"

People cheered, drinks were raised, "Just What I Needed" by the Cars thumped back to full volume.

"Those guys are lucky, man!"

"Or *un*lucky."

"Two hours with Theresa."

"To Theresa!"

"Hear Hear!"

"And to Crackerbox Mansion, and Connie and Elaine and Pamela!"

"Yeah!"

"I couldn't live in this shit-hole town without these parties."

"You said it, man."

The music continued, people danced and swayed and drank and smoked, they coupled and uncoupled and recoupled. The corners of each room accumulated piles of clothes. The ceiling above the large front room vibrated with thuds, and even above the stereo the voice of Nurse Theresa boomed.

"The Bishop wishes for you to increase your pace!"

"I — can't go any fast—"

"And your depth! Increase your depth! Both of you!"

"Oh — God —"

The revelers in the front room paused their own movements to look up at the ceiling.

"Did she just say 'both of you'?"

"Indeed she did."

"Damn."

"Yes Yes Yes! Ahahaaaaha. Ahhhhh!"

"The Bishop wishes for you to maintain silence during the liturgy!"

"I— submit — to the wishes —"

"SILENCE!"

Wham Wham Wham, then a crash.

"What the hell are they doing up there?"

"It's like they're rearranging the furniture."

"I don't even want to know what they're doing."

"I do."

"Yeah, so do I."

The night deepened. Candles and incense were lit. Windows were opened to let in cooler air. The smells and sounds and funk of Crackerbox Mansion wafted out the windows and floated up into the dark sky, through the trees and down the empty neighborhood streets of Paxton. And there along the sidewalk on Cornwall Street walked a small priest, quietly making his way toward the house.

Father Bennett had lived at the nearby parish rectory for many years and was accustomed to neighbor complaints about Crackerbox Mansion. As he approached the house, he heard whooping and tromping, and from every open window there was loud laughing and rock music and wisps of smoke. Father Bennett chuckled softly. None of this bothered him a bit — after all, he himself had been somewhat of a beatnik in his younger days before entering the priesthood. He'd had a beard and a full head of hair and smoked a pipe and had attended concerts by The Weavers and had very nearly enrolled in the Old Town School of Folk Music in Chicago. But those days were far behind him and now, as he reached the large red front door of the party house, he was clean-shaven and wearing his black shirt and priest's collar, having just returned from visiting a sick parishioner at Rockland County Hospital at the other end of Cornwall Street. There hadn't been time to change before Mrs. Walters knocked on the rectory door to implore him to please go talk to those awful hippie neighbors again about their house of pandemonium. So here he was now.

He banged on the iron knocker and the door swung immediately open. A young man wearing a brown monk's robe smiled and stretched his arms wide.

"Crackerbox Mansion welcomes you!"

"Yes, good evening," said the priest. "My name is Father B—"

"Heeeey, a priest costume. Fucking awesome! You can call me Mike — Mike the Monk."

"Yes, well —"

"Come in, come in." Mike the Monk held the door wide and gestured to let the priest into the house.

"I was actually concerned about all the noise here. One

of our neighbors asked me to stop by and — oh, what's that?"

They both looked up, where through the open windows above the porch the sounds of the Bishop's game were in full force.

"Ahhhhh — what are you doing — that is so — Oh My G— Ahhhhhh!"

Mike the Monk smiled. "Yeah, Theresa is the Bishop tonight, and we all know what that means."

Father Bennett smiled at Mike.

Mike looked back at the priest.

The father blinked once, then twice.

Mike glanced down at Father Bennett's collar, then back up at his eyes. "Oh my god, you're actually — you're an actual —" and he slammed the front door.

Father Bennett sighed and considered knocking again, then walked along the porch and glanced in through one of the front room windows. He gasped at the kaleidoscope before him.

Tangles of nude bodies in various positions on chairs and couches and even against the wall, incense smoke and "Slow Ride" by Foghat, two men busy with one woman on a recliner. Nurse Elaine was wearing a nun's habit and was sauntering through the room tossing out handfuls of condoms from a basket hooked over her forearm. Leaned back in a chair directly in front of the window lounged a naked long-haired bearded man with his back to Father Bennett; on the floor before him knelt a woman whose head was repeatedly thrusting downward onto his lap. On the couch next to them lay a nude couple side-by-side, their hands enmeshed with each other's genitals. Nurse Elaine stopped to kiss one of them long and hard before continuing her procession into the next room.

Father Bennett's eyes could not have been wider. He glanced from the couple to the man sitting to the kneeling woman and then to the nun who was exiting the room with her basket. The smoke and the music and the howling and banging from upstairs all made him feel a bit nauseated.

The nude man with his back to the window sat up rigid and said, "Good good good good good good uuuhhhhhhh" and then collapsed backward into the seat. After a few more moments, the woman kneeling in front of him tossed her hair sideways as she sat upright and tipped her head back to swig from a beer bottle. Father Bennett watched the woman guzzle and then tilt her head back down. She glanced up to the window and saw the priest. Their gazes locked — and Father Bennett realized he was staring directly into the eyes of Mrs. Prichard. Her jaw dropped. Father Bennett clutched his chest. He felt a sharp pain in his left arm and pressed his chest harder then dropped to the porch floor with a thump.

"Ohmygod Ohmygod, Hey!" yelled Mrs. Prichard. "On the porch! Out there! Help him!"

Everyone threw on clothes, rushed outside, and gathered around Father Bennett.

"Oh shit."

"What happened?"

"Who is that?"

"He fell."

"Oh crap, is he breathing?"

"Call an ambulance!"

"Someone get Connie!"

Nurse Connie shoved through with a first-aid bag. "Lookout lookout lookout."

She knelt down next to the priest and started CPR.

Above them, the thrashing and slamming continued.

"Someone get upstairs and tell them to stop."

"I'm not going up there."

"Yeah, are *you* going to tell Theresa to stop?"

"Not me, man."

Connie continued CPR on the priest for many minutes. The rhythm of her chest compressions was synchronized with screams of "Uh Uh Uh Uh" from the room above. The upstairs moans grew louder as Bishop Theresa yelled "Harder, dammit! Harder!" culminating in two ecstatic screams as the priest gasped and revived, and everyone on the porch applauded and cheered.

Flashing red and yellow lights illuminated the front of the house as the Rockland County Volunteer Rescue Squad ambulance parked on the sidewalk and two paramedics — Brad and Susan — jumped out. They jogged up to the porch and tended to Father Bennett. He was dazed but conscious.

The room upstairs went quiet.

Mike the Monk glanced upward. "Are they done?"

But then a slow thumping began again.

Josh the Bosh looked at his watch. "Nope, they've got ten more minutes."

The thumping now mixed with shrieking and cracking.

"What the hell sound is that?"

Brad the paramedic looked up from the patient. "Wow," he said. "Who's the bishop tonight?"

"Theresa."

"Oh god," said Brad. "Maybe we should stick around. How many acolytes?"

"Three."

"Okay, that's safer than two."

"You would know, Brad!"

"Oh man, would I ever." Brad stared stunned at the porch ceiling.

Susan the paramedic was ready to move the patient.

"Brad! Your partner wishes for you to focus!"

"Right, sorry." Brad helped lift the priest onto the gurney.

They walked the stretcher to the ambulance, hoisted Father Bennett into the back, then drove off.

The ambulance rolled away down Cornwall Street. People drifted back into the house. A group of partyers stayed on the porch, bottles were passed around, lighters and matches were lit. Other people congregated in the dining room as Josh the Bosh opened a cooler and handed out popsicles.

There was silence upstairs and then slow tromping down the back staircase. The three boys were covered in sweat, spent, exhausted, as they staggered down into the dining room and were applauded by the congregation. The boys removed their purple tunics and hung them on the coat rack. They drank water, oceans of water. People handed them popsicles and slapped their backs.

"Wow, you guys were up there for a long time."

"Two hours, man, we did it! We survived!"

"What did you do up there?"

"You gotta put on a tunic and find out for yourself."

"I'm scared."

"You should be."

"But I mean, how bad could it be?"

The three boys laughed and laughed.

Bishop Theresa had reclothed herself and now descended the stairs to the cheering throng, waving and holding a small basket. She reached into the basket and flung a handful of empty condom wrappers at the crowd like the homecoming queen on a parade float.

"Count them! Count them!"

"Holy Shit, this could be a new record."

Two partyers scrambled around on the floor collecting the wrappers, then spread them on the dining room table into a grid, four rows of five.

"Twenty total, damn."

"No way, impossible. There were only three of you."

"Ah," said one of the boys, "but they weren't all used by us."

"What?"

"Some of them were used *on* us."

"Oh my God, the Holy Dildo Scepter?"

"Yep. Several."

"Oh."

The boys clinked their popsicles together, toasting each other three-Musketeers style.

Meanwhile across town, just over the railroad tracks on Monroe Street, Richard Prichard was spending a quiet evening at home. The ambulance call came through on his Radio Shack scanner in the living room, but he missed it because at that moment he was upstairs putting the children to bed. Twenty minutes later, he came back downstairs and poured himself a glass of Johnnie Walker on the rocks, ready for a few blissful hours of peace and relaxation. The kids were taken care of and his wife was at her friend Judy's house for their monthly game of bridge. My, how his wife loved that game. He settled into his recliner and turned up the volume on the scanner just in time to hear Brad the paramedic radio that the patient was stable and they were transporting him to the hospital. And when Mr. Prichard heard the address they were leaving, he froze mid-sip. It was that damned house on Cornwall Street. He gently put his glass down and stood straight up, enough is enough. He locked the house on his way out, jumped into his Cadillac Seville, drove to Crackerbox Mansion, and parked on the street right next to a Volvo station wagon he didn't even notice. He crashed through the gate and into the front yard, yelling at the assembly of people smoking and drinking on the porch.

"An ambulance? Really? Did someone go too far? Just what happened here?"

"Aw man, it's him."

"I'm going to have this place shut down!"

Josh the Bosh ambled down the front porch steps to meet Mr. Prichard on the front walk. "Dude, chill out man."

"We're shutting it down!"

"What do you mean shutting it down? It's a private residence, man."

And then Richard Prichard looked over Josh's shoulder and saw Mrs. Prichard in the crowd on the front porch, wearing a fringed red corset that hugged the curves of her petite frame. Mr. Prichard's eyes froze wide, he stood rigid, catatonic. He pushed Josh aside and walked slowly to the porch steps.

All talking stopped, everyone watched Richard Prichard.

He stood looking at Mrs. Prichard, his head tilted to the right. He raised a hand and extended a finger and pointed at his wife, then slowly scanned his finger at all the people on the porch. His body began quivering.

Josh the Bosh walked up behind him and put a hand on his shoulder. "Hey man, it's okay."

Mr. Prichard waved his arm with a rigid index finger, holding his breath, his face reddening, his hair dancing.

"Gaaaaahhhhhhhh! You! You!" He pointed at his wife. "This — Gaaaaaahhhh."

Mrs. Prichard had the tiniest smile on her face as she calmly sipped from her glass.

"Judy's house!" said Mr. Prichard. "What about bridge at Judy's house?"

And then his eyes moved right and he saw Judy right there on the porch smoking a joint, a hirsute hippie's arm around her shoulders.

"This— this — Gaaaaahhhhhh!"

Everyone else was silent. The only sound was Mr. Prichard's fast breathing. He dropped his arms to his sides. He looked at his wife and spoke in a low growl. "Darling. You are coming home now."

All eyes turned to Mrs. Prichard, who stared at her husband with her mouth still turned up in a slight smile. One hand lifted her drink to her cherry-red lips while the other was planted firmly on the curve of her left hip.

"And take off that outfit!" Mr. Prichard's eyes tracked down along his wife's bare legs and landed on her shimmering ruby high heels. He gulped. And then he whispered, "Those shoes. I've never seen —" He looked back up at her face. "Just how long have you been —"

"Oh, Richard." Judy was shaking her head.

"Quiet Quiet Quiet Quiet Quiet!" Spit sprayed from Mr. Prichard's mouth. "Get down here now!"

The crowd on the porch parted down the middle as Nurse Theresa emerged through the front door, still wearing the high Bishop's miter. She stood next to Mrs. Prichard.

Richard Prichard pointed. "You!"

Mrs. Prichard glanced at Theresa and then up at the tall hat. "May I?"

Theresa smiled. She reached up with both hands, lifted

the Bishop's hat, and gently lowered it onto the head of Mrs. Prichard.

This caused an immediate and intense scramble as multiple people pushed each other and lurched for the coat rack to fight for the purple tunics. In the end, three lucky acolytes emerged victorious: two men and one woman.

Mr. Prichard's confused gaze went from the swarming throng to the tunics to Theresa, and to his wife who was now holding a long pole of some kind, and my God, what was that at the top of it?

"Darling, enough of this," he said. "You are coming with me now."

Mrs. Prichard handed her drink to a bystander and turned away toward the front door of Crackerbox Mansion.

"Now! You come with me now, or don't *ever* come home again."

Her high heels clicked on the wooden porch floor as she disappeared into the house, the three acolytes following solemnly behind her.

About the Author

Robert Slentz-Kesler is a librarian whose fiction has appeared in *Litro Magazine*, the *Blotter, the Rappahannock Review, the Font, All About Jazz,* and the *Brussels Review.* When not voraciously seeking out and promoting banned books, he spends time drinking espresso and reading Scandinavian crime novels. He lives and writes in Durham, North Carolina. See more of his work at www.robertslentzkesler.com.

COMMENT SECTION

JIM RULAND

First of all, I just want to say how awful this is and my heart goes out to the friends and families of the victims. What happened out there is heartbreaking.... But I don't know how someone could write a story like this and be so blasé about the deaths of four young people. This is why people don't trust the media anymore. There's obviously more going on here than your typical drug overdose story... a lot more!

....

Thank you for saying this. I never expected something like this would happen to Anna. RIP.

....

Never do drugs alone.

....

Read the article stupid. They weren't alone. There were four of them. That's why this is so messed up.

....

Exactly! One person overdosing is an accident but four people dying is a crime.

....

Those of you who are leaving cruel comments are monsters. Imagine if your child died like this! Or if you're too young to have children, what if your brother or sister or boyfriend or girlfriend died under "mysterious circumstances" and the only thing the police will tell you is the investigation is ongoing? Friends and family members who are trying to make sense of this tragedy read these comments. Think about that! Think about how that would make you feel!

....

You're right... It's not cool to joke around like that. My friend died from a Viagra overdose and his wife took it real hard.

....

Guys, this story is fake AF. There is no Dreamcatcher, CA. It's not on Google maps. It's not on Apple maps. It doesn't exist. TBH I wouldn't be surprised if the band was behind it as some kind of publicity stunt.

....

The first rule of Dreamcatcher is there is no Dreamcatcher.

....

I didn't want to write this but my name is Patricia and Brandon Alvarez was my cousin. I'm tired of seeing Brandon and his friends referred to as "the deceased" or "the victims." They had names! Brandon Alvarez, Anna Lee, Carlos Castillos and Amelia Bondurant. I didn't really know the others but I feel like I did because me and Brandon were close and I was friends with some of his friends on social media. Like I said Brandon was my cousin and he lived with my family his junior year because he was having trouble at home that I won't get into but it wasn't drug related, OK? He was the sweetest guy and I was honestly sad when he went back to live with his mom after his dad moved out at the end of the year and I didn't see him as much. We worked together at the CVS on Valley Vista. He was a good worker and everyone liked him, even the customers. He wasn't the type to cause drama. Brandon would party a little bit. Nothing too serious. Just beer and weed. I'm not trying to make him look bad or anything I just think that some of the things people are saying about him are way off. He wasn't a drug dealer. I never saw him do hard drugs just weed like I said. That's not to say he didn't do some that night, but I never saw it, and it would surprise me if he did. I know it's everywhere these days, but he just wasn't into that, which makes this whole thing even sadder. I know for some of you this is a weird story to get excited about like it's a TV show or something but Brandon and his friends were regular people and they didn't deserve to die like this.

....

Who was the band?

....

Blatant Stereotypes. OG punks from back in the day.

....

OG mall punk maybe.

....

Blatant Stereotypes suck.

....

What use is language when you can look to the stars, the universe mapped in righteous symmetry?

....

That's deep bruh. You ever get so high you scare yourself?

....

I just want to say that I wasn't there but I think Anna had a premonition about what was going to happen to her but again I wasn't there.

....

Or maybe Anna knew something that we don't.

....

Someone posted a video from inside the house from before the incident. It's like a real estate tour or something? This lady is going on and on about all of the amenities and when they get to the room where they found the bodies the lady gets quiet and the video gets slightly darker. When I watched it again there's like a shadow that passes in front of the camera lens. I don't know if it's a glitch or a negative energy thing but just from watching that video you can feel that something is very, very wrong in that house.

....

FTS are cheap and easy to get. Naloxone is your friend.

....

Friends don't let friends do untested drugs.

....

Hear me out. What if it was some kind of a sacrifice? Think about it. The article says these friends were found in a circle, which is weird because who sits like that? No one unless it was some kind of ritual. But what if they were placed in a circle AFTER they died? We're not talking about a circle anymore. We're talking about a cross. That doesn't sound so innocent. That sounds like a Solar Cross to me. Look it up. This is some real-deal sacred geometry we're dealing with and the wild thing is we don't know what these kids thought they were getting into but if these bodies were arranged AFTER they died then there was definitely something freaky going down.

....

Some of you get your witchcraft from the internet and it shows.

....

I stayed in that house and the only thing weird about it is how far away from everything it is. There are a couple of other houses out there but the only business is a bar that looks like no one's been inside for a million years but when you look in the window it's fully furnished with beer signs on the wall. There's even a pool table. It's like it shut down last week. Nothing happened while I stayed in the house but I had the strangest dreams that made no sense and I woke up in a pool of sweat, my heart racing. After that, I felt like I had to leave. I didn't even take a shower. I just packed my shit and left.

....

Sounds like a COVID dream, dude.

....

Okay this is weird I was looking around Airbnb and the house isn't there anymore. They scrubbed it. Either the owner delisted it or Airbnb took it down. I can see making it unavailable for rental but to take the whole thing down seems strange to me.

....

It was fentanyl. There I solved the case. Do I get a reward?

....

Definitely fent. If you don't have a tolerance for that shit it's good night forever. Those saying it wouldn't happen that quickly don't know what they're talking about.

....

OMG I went to school with Amelia and she was the coolest ever. We had Algebra together with Mr. Mohr who was a total dick and she let me copy off her even though I could tell she didn't want to not because she was a prude or anything but because she wanted to go to college and cheating is cheating. Someone told me she liked Takis Ranch Rolls and I bought a bunch of bags that I kept in my locker and I kept giving them to her in class and after school and it became this running joke between us and that's how we become friends. I can't believe she's gone.

....

Someone should reach out to the band and let them know what happened. I'm sure they'd be interested to know that four of their fans died.

....

Blatant Stereotypes has fans in their 20s? LOL!

....

Four trustafarians OD at a music festival called Dreamcatcher? Cry me a river. Maybe the spirits of the Mojave people have a sense of humor after all

....

Dreamcatcher isn't like that. It's a dumb name but they made it that way on purpose. It's a small DIY music and arts festival but not in the traditional sense. Totally underground, super down low kind of deal. My bestie's sister did a temporary sculpture out there last year and she had to sign all these contracts saying she wouldn't promote the show or put anything on social media or she'd forfeit her artwork. The organizers didn't want it to turn into this corporate influencer shitshow for the 1%. So I get why people are pissed at Blatant Stereotypes for posting a flyer of the show. Those kids weren't supposed to be there. They weren't even supposed to know about it. If the band had just played by the rules those kids would still be alive.

....

OMG! Anna Lee RIP. So tragic!

....

Some of you commenting on this story act like these kids were found in some crack shack in the middle of nowhere. It was an Airbnb with a hot tub and a fireplace. It's probably nicer than where a lot of you keyboard detectives live.

....

Does anyone know if any of these people were dating or involved with each other?

....

I'm freaking out right now. When I heard this story about four punkers dying in the desert I knew Carlos C. was one of them. I just knew. I don't mean to speak ill of the dead but that dude was bad news. That fool has been causing trouble at parties and shows since forever. He was always mixed up with people who were into heavy shit. Always. If that's your thing, cool, just keep it away from me and keep it away from the scene where that kind of thing can have a negative impact on people who don't want it there. Maybe back in the day people did that shit at shows and no one said anything but this isn't back in the day. Its 2023 and people are just trying to survive. Some of us have been struggling since before the pandemic. I feel like if you make drama for people ultimately that shit comes back on you and it looks like it came back on Carlos in a big way. I just hope the other people involved didn't go down because of him but this gives me a bad, bad feeling. I don't know if cops read these things for clues but homeboy was into some shady shit that needs to be looked into.

....

OK narc.

....

People OD every day. What makes these shitheads so special?

....

For real. My brother died from a fentanyl overdose two years ago and my uncle ODed the year before that. My sister was like enough is enough I'm calling the news, I'm calling the newspapers, I'm calling that dude who does the local breaking news on Tik Tok. This shit has got to stop. People need to know they are straight up killing us with that shit out here. Guess how many stories they did about my brother? If you guessed zero you guessed right. They were like nah, we good. They call it an epidemic but they don't care about us. They really don't.

....

The media is trying so hard to sensationalize the story. As soon as they find out these kids overdosed they'll drop it.

....

Check this out. I was at a show a couple weeks ago. It was more of a party than a show but there were a bunch of bands. This dude built a skate ramp in his back yard and his parents made him take it down because they didn't want to be liable for any accidents so he threw a party and invited a bunch of bands and afterwards everyone tore the ramp down. Hella fun. There was an old dude there that was talking to some of the women at the party, said he had some shit for sale, very good price, blah blah blah. Turns out they found one of those women in the bathroom after the show and she was fucking blue. Whoever found her was able to bring her back and it was a gnarly scene. I guess the moral of the story is don't take drugs from strangers but when I heard about what went down in Dreamcatcher I immediately thought of this dude.

....

Here's a thought. Instead of lecturing us about testing drugs and getting Narcan training, what if we, you know, didn't do the drugs in the first place? Wouldn't that solve a lot of problems? Everyone knows we're in the middle of an opioid epidemic. Ok whatever. What do you think is happening where these drugs are being made? What about the harm that's being done in those communities? I'm not trying to tell people what to do but that shit is bad news all around and maybe, just maybe, we'd all be better off as a society if we just didn't do them. I'm not talking about people with chronic illnesses. I'm not talking about people experiencing homelessness. I'm not talking about people with brain health issues. I'm talking about recreational drug users in the punk rock community. We preach about safe spaces and looking out for each other but turn our head when the white powder comes out. How does that make sense?

....

You ARE telling people what to do. They make fent in factories so spare us the social justice lecture.

....

This is on Blatant Stereotypes. I used to like them but they own this.

....

I don't see how you can read all this and not understand that Blatant Stereotypes had nothing to do with what went on out there. They didn't play. They weren't even there.

....

No one's talking about the blood on the door.

....

So Dreamcatcher is some kind of secret society or something? You can show your art or play your music but you can't tell anyone about it? What kind of shit is that? There's something super cult-y about that if you ask me. If this happened to someone in my family I'd lawyer up.

....

Dreamcatcher is a CONCEPT. You can't prosecute an IDEA.

....

This is why you don't have music festivals without proper protocols. Everyone is anti-corporation these days. But who do think pays for the security? Who pays for the paramedics when someone needs medical attention? Who pays for the porta potties and the water stations and the insurance? Corporate sponsors, that's who. No one likes rules. No one likes people telling them what to do especially at a concert or a show. But those rules keep people safe. Without rules you get anarchy. If you're okay with that then you don't get to complain when shit doesn't go according to plan.

....

News flash: corporate rock sucks.

....

I have a friend who used to be a paramedic in the high desert and he had the craziest stories. He had to quit because he couldn't handle all the deaths. He said they spent most of their time treating the same addicts over and over and over again. It got to where he felt like someone died every time he took a day off.

....

That's why you don't fuck around out there in the desert.

....

I'm sorry but most of you don't understand Dreamcatcher. You wish you were cool enough or rich enough to go to Coachella or Burning Man but you aren't and you carry those negative feelings inside you. Did you know you can create your own Coachella? There's nothing stopping you from throwing your own shows, making your own scene. Most you don't even understand that's an option. You just want to buy things. Can you imagine a show without Ticketmaster or Live Nation or even credit cards? You probably can't. Can you imagine going to a show without your phone? I bet you can't. That's what Dreamcatcher was. No one owned it. No one sold tickets. No one was in charge. Just pure energy, pure expression, and it was awesome. It was the only place in California that was truly free and Blatant Stereotypes fucking ruined it. By posting a flyer on the internet, they attracted people to Dreamcatcher who 100% didn't belong there. Those kids tried to buy their way into a scene they didn't participate in. That doesn't make them bad people, they didn't know any better, and guess what? The desert has a way of showing you just how little you know.

....

DIY or die.

....

I guess they chose death.

....

If you're wondering why there are no arrests in this case it's because not everything is a conspiracy. No one made those kids do drugs. They knew the risks.

....

Everyone is just assuming it's drugs and it's making me crazy. Did the police say it was drugs? Did their families? If you listen to the families they are saying it's NOT drugs. Has anyone here seen a toxicology report? No, you haven't so STFU. Someone did this to them!

....

When the fourth sign was laid the angel carvers were unleashed.

....

If they were like murdered or something what if the killer is reading these comments? What if they're reading them right now?

....

OK I wasn't going to say anything. I swear I've written this and deleted it at least five times. I work with Anna Lee at High Desert Drip in Cabazon. It's only been open a couple months so maybe you haven't seen it but that's not important. Like I said I work with Anna and I can't believe she's gone. We have a lot of the same shifts and I like working with her because she's really pretty and I always get way more tips when I work with Anna even though we're never really crazy busy. We never get super slammed except maybe when big groups come in and then the shift goes by really fast. What I'm saying is we have a lot of down time and talk to each other about all kinds of stuff and I would say we know each other really well even though we have totally different taste in music and guys and whatever. I like the girly girl stuff like Billie Eilish and Olivia Rodrigo and Lana del Rey though I'm not that into Lana anymore and Anna is into stuff that I would say is more aggressive. Not like scary aggressive but in your face like Blatant Stereotypes. That was her favorite band. If you ask me what my favorite band is sometimes it's Billie, sometimes it's Olivia, but Anna wasn't like that. Blatant Stereotypes was always her favorite. I guess the band has been having problems and they haven't been playing as much so when Anna found out they were coming to the desert she was so excited which you'd understand if you lived out here. She put in her request to get that weekend off and made plans with her crew that she told me she mostly knew from online but had spent time with at other shows in the past. Anna told me the Airbnb was super dope and super expensive. She showed me pictures on her phone and it looked really nice. I was genuinely happy for her. I'm sorry I know this seems like I'm rambling but it's important you know how excited she was and how much she'd planned and how hard she'd worked to make it happen because the day before she left she was super down. Like I took one look at her and I knew something was seriously wrong. We spent too much time together to be able to hide our feelings from each other. Maybe that makes me an empath or something but Anna was the same way with me. I'm getting choked up writing this because when Anna said "Hey, are you okay?" it didn't matter if I was going through some things at home with my sister and her kid who live with me because she's not working right now or some customer was being mean to me, she put her energy into my feelings and that's a quality not a lot of people have. She was more than just a coworker to me. The day before she left she came into work looking like something terrible had happened. I just asked her straight up, "What happened?" And guys I'm being real with you about this stuff about me and Anna and where we worked and everything because I'm putting it out there exactly the way it happened and she said. "I don't want to go to Dream-catcher. I feel like something bad is going to happen." Those were her exact words. I'm not making this up or being dramatic. I asked her if something was wrong with the Airbnb or her car because sometimes she had car trouble but she said, "No, I just don't want to go." We talked about it all day. She didn't want to go but felt like she had to because it was so expensive and it would be even more expensive for the others if she backed out at the last minute. I told her if you feel so strongly about it don't go and I even thought about offering to help cover the cost of the rental because I'd never seen her so down before and she'd been so excited about this trip but with three people in the house my bills have gone up but whatever she decided I wanted her to be okay with it but at the end of her shift when she left she looked even worse than when she came in. She hugged me goodbye and it was awful and thinking about it now I honestly believe she knew she was never coming back and she wasn't going to see me again. I'm sorry if that's upsetting for people to read. I'm sorry if you think I'm being dramatic. I'm sorry if you think I'm throwing Anna under the bus but I'm not. With everything that happened I feel like it's important for people to know what her mental state was before she went to Dreamcatcher. I really do.

. . . .

We love you Anna. 🖤

About the Author

Jim Ruland is an old punk who lives by the sea. He is the author of the novels *Make It Stop* and *Forest of Fortune* and the short story collection *Big Lonesome*. He is also the *LA Times* bestselling author of *Corporate Rock Sucks: The Rise & Fall of SST Records*, which was named a Best Book of 2022 by *Pitchfork, Rolling Stone,* and *Vanity Fair*. Ruland is the co-author of *Do What You Want* with Bad Religion and *My Damage* with Keith Morris. Jim is a frequent contributor to *Razorcake* fanzine and the *LA Times*. He is a veteran of the U.S. Navy and lives in San Diego.

HOW TO PSYCHO-ANALYZE YOURSELF

FLEUR BRADLEY

HARRY WAS JUST TAGGING along on his wife's rummage sale run that Saturday. They were at an outdoor flea market, on a nice sunny day. It wasn't too busy, so he didn't mind. Still, he'd rather be putting his feet up after a long week teaching uninterested high school kids.

But that sun made the outing nice. He felt the knot between his shoulders soften. Truth was, things had been tense around the house lately. There were money squabbles, sure, but not enough to account for the distance he felt between himself and his wife. Lately, Amy was always after things to do, a reason to look somewhere other than in his eyes.

Harry had actually considered that she might be having an affair. So, when she'd suggested spending the day at this flea market, Harry agreed to come along.

Amy was up ahead a few stalls, examining a dilapidated dresser. It was what she did: fix things, glue them back, then sand and varnish or paint until you couldn't see the break anymore. Not new, but better than new. Amy was a fixer.

Harry stepped closer to a nearby stall with books. There

were boxes of them, marked a couple of dollars, some a few more. There was one other customer there looking, but he quickly moved along. Perhaps another husband, killing time while his wife shopped. *How very old-fashioned*, Harry thought to himself. Amy was always telling him he was, and one of the kids in his class once called him old-school. Harry took it as a compliment.

Just as he was ready to move along, his eyes drifted to a box full of tiny books, pocket-sized. They looked more like stapled booklets. Harry resisted the urge to pick one up. The paper was yellowed and old, and it looked like they'd all turn to dust any minute. He browsed the titles with his hands behind his back, observing only.

Facts You Should Know About Animal Life

A History of Evolution

But also, stories by Edgar Allen Poe, and various classic authors.

"Those are Little Blue Books. They're from the nineteen-twenties," the woman behind the table said. Her voice was gravelly, a heavy smoker, her skin sallow and her gray hair frizzy. "Some got stories, others got advice and such. Sized to fit in your pocket, real handy. Collectable, they are."

Harry nodded to be polite. Despite himself, he lifted a booklet, and saw a title that made him smile.

How to Psycho-Analyze Yourself by Daniel H. Bonus, *Little Blue Book No. 651* it said at the top.

"Careful," the woman said.

"How much?" he heard himself ask.

"Thirty for the bundle," the woman said. You could tell she knew she was pushing it. But it was a flea market after all. You'd start high, if you were selling.

"Just this one." Harry lifted the little book. He wanted it now.

The woman knew it. "Ten."

"I'll give you five," Harry said, thinking he was overpaying but wanting to wrap it up before Amy saw him. He wasn't sure why.

The woman quickly took the five-dollar bill when he passed it.

Harry tucked away the Little Blue Book, inside his flannel shirt's front pocket. Just before Amy motioned him over to carry the dresser to the van.

Question 14: Are you definite or vague of purpose?

Harry had been thumbing through the Little Blue Book, smiling to himself as he read the questions. There were several pages of them, then there were answers in the last half or so of the thing. Now this was truly old-fashioned. But he tucked the booklet away when he heard his wife join him in the kitchen. It was his little secret. One he wanted to keep, especially since he suspected Amy had her own secret.

"It's been quiet over at the Jones's house," Harry said to Amy as she sat down at the breakfast table with her coffee mug. The kitchen of their small house looked out over the garden, and at the back of the Jones's house. He hadn't minded that when he and Amy first moved in, that they were looking right at their neighbors' sizably bigger abode than theirs. Harry loved his house, was proud of it. But over the years he saw the disparity, and it had started to get under his skin.

Now the Joneses were redoing their back garden, with the trees and flowers already removed. Pavers were stacked to the side, and a hole had been dug to pour the concrete base for a giant fountain. Excess, Harry thought.

Harry and Amy were both teachers with modest salaries — that they'd been able to afford this house, in this neighborhood, had been a lucky break. It was a fixer, a former guest house to the bigger structure that the Joneses lived in.

It didn't feel like such a lucky break anymore, when he saw that big house every time he sat at his kitchen table. And they saw other things from their house. Things Harry wished he didn't.

Domestics, his friend Greg, a police officer, called them. Arguments between husband and wife. At first, they were just screaming matches. But eventually the fights became violent. Once, Harry had called Greg. And there had been the home visit from a patrol car. After that, the curtains were drawn more often than not.

But you could still hear them.

"Maybe they sorted things out," Amy suggested. She looked on edge.

"Unlikely." Harry had grown up in a violent household. It didn't end, he knew from experience. Not unless someone left, like his mother had, going back to her native Arizona. Like his friend Greg said over their Sunday afternoon beer, in extreme cases one of the parties wound up dead.

He wasn't sure if it was the tiny book or his wife's hooded eyes that spurred him on, but Harry decided to be bold. "I'm going over there to check."

Amy started to argue, but he ignored her. The outside air was comfortably brisk as Harry traversed the torn-up garden. His father, a career gardener with a successful landscaping business who was appreciative of mature plants, would not approve. Harry shrugged those thoughts aside and knocked on the back door. While he waited, he felt his boldness fade, like it had leaked out of him on his walk.

The door opened. "Harry." Camilla had a tired smile, but

her face looked fine — no cuts or bruises. However, like Greg would say: a talented abuser knows where to hit so no one sees the damage.

"Just wanted to check if you were okay," Harry said. He looked over his shoulder, but couldn't see Amy because the sun reflected off their kitchen window.

"Fine, yeah. Dom is out of town on business." She gave him a little smile, but a nervous one. "He's been gone for a few days now."

Harry nodded. "We're here if you need anything."

The door closed before he could say anything else. Harry turned and looked at the garden under construction. That big fountain would block the view to his and Amy's house. And from their house to the Jones's, too.

So they could hide.

Question 47: Are you trustful or suspicious?

The rest of that Sunday got eaten up by errands, and cooking and cleaning. In the evening, they did a little TV watching. Amy turned in early.

"Busy day tomorrow," she said with an exaggerated yawn. It was always busy when you were a teacher, but the coming week had testing on the schedule. Harry agreed and turned in early himself.

But he couldn't sleep. All he could think about was his mother's face, the tears that'd streaked her face when she finally got the courage to leave. Harry was already in college at the time and couldn't help her. Plus, he was working with his father whenever he could, doing landscaping to earn the money to finish school.

Dig. Dig, Harry. He'd been so proud to finish his college

degree, to provide Amy and their future kids with a better life than he'd had. But it was not enough, not anymore. He could see it in his wife's averted eyes.

Amy couldn't sleep either, it seemed, and around midnight she got up. Harry pretended to be sleeping while she slid into some jeans and a sweatshirt and zipped up her boots.

Where are you going, Amy?

Harry waited for his wife to go downstairs, then quickly followed.

In the kitchen, he saw her rush across the torn-up garden, then tap on the back door just like Harry had that very morning. Only this time, Camilla opened the door with a smile, and his wife gave her an embrace.

A very *long* embrace.

It took a moment, old-fashioned as Harry was, for the penny to drop.

Question 66: Are you fanciful or over-imaginative?

Amy came back after just an hour, but Harry knew there was a lot you could do in that time. In fact, as he was waiting for her — at first pacing their small living room, then sitting at the kitchen table — he remembered all the things *they* had done in the early years of their marriage, often in a lot less time. But there wasn't the passion anymore, fewer evening encounters like the one he was imagining his wife having now with their neighbor.

Wasn't that how a marriage worked, though? One of twelve years especially? One that had seen the ups and downs, like theirs — money troubles, job troubles, and unwanted childlessness?

In the small span of an hour, Harry tried consulting his Little Blue Book for answers, but there was no advice on wives having lesbian love affairs with neighbors, alas. So he thumbed through the booklet, answering questions to himself as he watched the light go on upstairs at the Jones's place, then turn back off some time later.

Did Dom know? He would probably kill Camilla if he did, Harry thought to himself. Then, secretly, he wished for his neighbor to come home — *surprise!* Harry imagined the ensuing argument, the screams. Then the flashing police lights as they arrested Dom and carted Camilla's body away on a stretcher.

It was amazing what you could dream up in just an hour.

Harry was too much of a coward to confront his wife, however. He just pretended to be asleep when she came in through the back door and folded herself back into their sheets. Amy smelled of soap.

Washing up after. Harry fumed all night next to her and well into the next day.

Question 31: Do you emphasize your dislike for sham?

That Monday was a blur of proctoring tests and pent-up anger for Harry. He could feel a scowl etched on his face until it hurt. By the time they had dinner, Harry thought he might throw his pot pie at his wife.

"I think I'm going to pop some dinner over to Camilla's," Amy said after she finished picking at hers. "She mentioned being under the weather the other day."

"When was that?" Harry asked.

Amy gave him a confused look. “Saturday. When we came home from the flea market.”

Harry nodded, sticking a bite of food in his mouth before he could say anything else. He watched Amy leave, wrapped dinner in hand, and walk across the garden.

After he did the dishes (breaking a glass, even), Harry couldn’t take it anymore. He stalked across the garden, and moved to rap his knuckles on the back door.

Then he thought better of announcing his visit. He reached for the doorknob.

It was unlocked.

The house smelled like stale air and a cleaning solution, or soap of some kind, as Amy had when she came home in the middle of the night. Harry first felt his anger ignite, then slowly dissipate as he checked the ground floor, the upstairs bedrooms, and eventually even the dark (and well-stocked) wine cellar.

But his wife wasn’t anywhere inside the lavishly decorated house. There was no sign of Camilla either. He was worried now. What if Dom had come back from his business trip, finding the two women in bed? Harry could imagine the man’s wrath. In fact Harry had, just the other night.

Confused, he eventually made his way through the mud room and to the door to the garage. He opened it. Carefully, slowly.

The overhead lights were on, harsh fluorescents bouncing off a perfectly finished garage floor, the kind Harry wished to have someday. There was a high-end Audi backed into the far-end space — Dom’s car, Harry knew. Another thing of his neighbor’s he coveted.

It wasn’t until he stepped into the garage that he saw the two women, near a large freezer that was tucked in the little alcove at the back of the garage. They both looked lost, upset.

And when they saw Harry, they looked horrified.

"Shit," Camilla said.

"Harry," Amy said softly, the way she always did when there was bad news. All those times the fertility treatment didn't work, and especially the last time, when their money ran out.

"He's dead, isn't he?" Harry asked, knowing it was a rhetorical question. Knowing his neighbor Dom was inside that freezer.

Question 24: How practical are you?

Camilla gave him a story that was all too familiar: there had been another argument, about how she parked her car this time. Dom made Camilla re-park it, again, and again, and again.

Only this time, Amy happened to be passing by. And like the fixer she was, she watched the scene unfold from the sidewalk. So she intervened.

"Nine times," Amy said, as they stood in the garage. "He made her repark her car *nine times*. And when it still wasn't good enough, he made her park outside."

So what? Harry wanted to ask, but then came the rest of the story. How Amy had confronted Dom. How he'd closed the garage door on her, trapping her inside while Camilla was outside, too afraid to get out of her car.

Then Dom had threatened Amy — punched her, even.

And Amy had grabbed the rake. Then she'd hit him on the head.

"He bled out," Amy said. "I didn't know what to do."

"We put Dom in the freezer," Camilla added in her soft voice.

Idiots, Harry thought but didn't say. All they would've had to do was call the police, and surely this would have been written up as self-defense. But it was too late now. Amy and Camilla had tried to cover it up.

Now they were stuck with this mess, with this body and a crime scene to clean up.

"We were going to drop him in the woods somewhere," Amy said, hands on her hips, just like she looked when it was time to load her furniture projects in the car.

"No," Harry said. "They can't ever find the body, or the police will come back here and find the crime scene. You have to bury him."

He sighed, watching their faces. Dom was a big guy. Harry knew, just like when loading the furniture, that Amy and Camilla would need his muscle. Old-fashioned, but true. Amy might be a fixer, but so was Harry.

He said, "We have to bury him. I know where."

Question 25: Can you use tools well?

Harry moved the rebar from where the fountain's concrete base was to be poured and used the shovel from Camilla's garage to dig a hole. He was reminded of his years landscaping with his father, a life he'd worked hard to get away from. All those years wielding a shovel so he could finish his degree. He might be old-fashioned, but he was breaking that family cycle of manual labor as a lifelong penance. Yet here he was, once again breaking up that unforgiving soil.

Dig. Dig, Harry.

It took hours but felt like days. Finally, they carried the body out back and into the grave. Harry didn't see a head wound but shrugged the whole thing off his sore back. It wasn't until Dom was buried and he put the rebar back on top of the soil that Harry exhaled.

The women stood, side-by-side, anxious as he handed Camilla back her shovel. There were giant red blisters on his palms and his fingers.

"Tomorrow the concrete is being poured, right?" Harry asked Camilla. He remembered the foreman talking about it, when Harry went over to talk to the landscaping crew while they took a break.

"Yes," she said softly, holding the shovel like it was a sharp knife.

Harry brushed the dirt off his jeans. "We'll move his car to an airport parking lot, one of those smaller places that don't have cameras."

They both nodded. In unison, which made Harry more uncomfortable than the fact that he'd just buried a dead body.

But again, he shrugged it off. In Camilla's kitchen, amid the custom cabinets and chef's appliances that cost more than his annual salary, they got their stories together. Dom had been distraught, Camilla would tell the police. He often talked of ending things. Once, he'd threatened to jump off a bridge. Amy and Harry would stay out of it all, but if questioned they would back up her story of a troubled, unhappy Dom.

Afterward, the women took off to drive the car to the airport.

"You've done enough Harry," Amy said, after giving him a quick peck on the cheek. "Go home."

Question 30: Are you honest with yourself?

The police came eventually, after Camilla filed a missing person's report. But Harry only got his information secondhand, from his wife. Mostly, Amy stayed away from the Joneses' house, just to keep them out of any suspicions. The police questioned Harry and Amy once, but it took all of five minutes before they were on their way.

Even a month later, it was quiet. Summer break was just around the corner, and Harry was going to be working for his father's landscaping business for some extra money. Amy would be teaching summer school. A few broken pieces of furniture sat forgotten in their guest room — Harry figured Amy didn't feel like fixing things anymore. They told each other that their summer jobs were to save up and move, but they both knew they could never leave. Not with the evidence of Amy's crime and Harry's complicity, staring right at them from that enormous fountain. They were trapped.

The Little Blue Book was forgotten, tossed onto his nightstand.

"What's this?" Amy had asked him a few days earlier. "*How to Psycho-Analyze Yourself*," she read with a smile. "Boy, you must be desperate."

He'd laughed, but couldn't really see the humor. And he didn't like how his wife had called him desperate, how she'd had this mocking tone. He'd covered up a murder for her. Buried a dead body — that was hardly desperate.

It was gallant, you might say. Especially if you considered that the story she and Camilla had told him didn't quite add up. Where were the wounds on Dom's head? And there had been no injuries on Amy that day. No bruises, or any other sign that Dom had been a threat.

Harry pretended none of it was happening. But sometimes his doubts popped up, like weeds through cracked concrete.

He took the booklet from Amy and placed it back on his nightstand.

That night, they turned in early. "Summer school," Amy said.

He nodded, thinking of the hard labor that was ahead for him. All the holes he had to dig. But Harry couldn't sleep. He thought of Dom, the way he'd been curled up in that freezer, and later in his grave — now under the giant fountain Harry saw out his kitchen window every day.

Question III: do you sleep well?

Harry rarely slept through the night anymore, making do with shards of fitful rest, leaving him exhausted most days. He'd sometimes sit in his kitchen, watching the water fall down the fountain's edges. Imagining Dom underneath, slowly decomposing. Who could rest, knowing what secret was right there, festering?

That night, apparently Amy couldn't sleep either. This time she waited until twelve-thirty to slip out of their bed. Harry imagined her passing the massive fountain and rapping softly on Camilla's back door. He couldn't see the Joneses' house anymore, not with that concrete monstrosity blocking his view. But Harry knew what was happening.

He thumbed through the Little Blue Book until the pages came away from the staples.

The next day, Greg came over to help Harry fix the dishwasher. Afterward, they were sitting in Harry's kitchen with a beer and some pizza.

"Whatever happened to your neighbors, the ones that had the domestic?" Greg asked.

"We don't really talk to them anymore," Harry said, explaining how Dom Jones had gone missing. "I'll bet he just took off. And I guess if he was beating his wife..." He let his voice trail off and the thought hang in the air, the one he'd been justifying his actions with: *the world was better off without Dom in it.*

Greg gave him a sideways glance. "*That's* what you thought?" He shook his head. "Nah, man. You know, it's not just husbands who beat wives. Sometimes, it's the other way around. You should've seen what Camilla Jones did to that man. And she knew just where to hit him too, where no one could see."

Harry felt himself go cold.

After Greg took another sip of his beer, he said, "You're old-school, Harry."

Harry didn't argue.

Then Greg pointed out the window, to the newly renovated garden. "Check out that giant fountain. It's sinking."

About the Author

Fleur Bradley has loved mysteries ever since she first picked up an Agatha Christie book at the age of eleven. She's the author of Agatha-nominated middle-grade mysteries *Daybreak on Raven Island* and *Midnight at the Barclay Hotel* (Viking/PRH), and the Double Vision trilogy (Harper-

Collins), as well as numerous non-fiction titles for the educational market.

Fleur started her writing journey many years ago, writing short crime fiction, and still enjoys writing in the short form. Most recently, her work has appeared in the MWA anthology *Super-Puzzletastic Mysteries*, SCBWI's *The Haunted States of America* (a story representing Colorado). *How to Teach Yourself to Swim*, originally published in Dark Yonder, was recently chosen for *The Best Mystery Stories of the Year 2024* anthology. Fleur's work has been nominated for the Agatha and Anthony Award and has won the Colorado Book Award and Colorado Authors League Book Award, among others.

A reluctant reader herself, Fleur is also a literacy advocate and speaks at events on how to reach reluctant readers. Originally from the Netherlands, she now lives in a small cottage in the foothills of the Colorado Rockies where she fosters rescue animals. You can find Fleur online at fleur-bradley.com.

THE GOLDEN AGE FALLACY

CW BLACKWELL

SHE'D BEEN PUSHING herself every night, a growing sleep-debt she couldn't repay even in a month's time, and now the hallucinations had taken hold. They would come soon after the bar closed, as she worked alone to settle the register, or when she mopped the grime from the wood laminate — vague night shapes hunkering on barstools, grim faces regarding her from the back wall, phantom rats drowning in the sludge of her mop bucket. She knew they weren't real. She knew the three or four hours she spent lying horizontal between workdays had starved her brain of dreams and now her dreams had come calling.

But the figments felt real enough and sometimes she'd curse them.

"Last call was thirty minutes ago," she'd say to the ghosts. *"Get the fuck out."*

Some late night in March, after she'd locked and alarmed the door and was crossing Knight Street toward Pacific Avenue, she noticed a man lying on his back, starfished over the cold sidewalk. She'd spotted him beneath the town clock, where others lay curled in tarps and sleeping bags with their beanies pulled low and bottles hid away in their pockets. It was the corduroy jacket with patches on the elbow that caught her eye — that, and the silver, shaggy hair.

"John?" she called. "John Braun?"

She often carried a knife ring when she walked home at night, a hard plastic claw like some twisted token of love. She fitted it over her knuckle and went slowly to the sprawled man.

"John, is that you?"

She wondered if this, too, was another waking dream — but they were never quite this real. She bent down and swept the hair from his face. Two swollen purple eyes above a clotted nose. He reeked of booze and blood and vomit, and there was a dark, scummy stain beneath his head that might have consisted of all three. She patted his cheeks and spoke his name. His face felt warm, his neck pliant. She rolled him onto his side and he sputtered and retched.

"I'm calling an ambulance," she said, slipping her phone from her pocket. Another man folded a corner of his tarp and looked around as if the word *ambulance* made him wary. The sleepers of the town clock didn't like emergency vehicles of any kind. "You're hurt bad. Jesus, I thought you were dead."

"No," he said, and retched again. "No ambulance. Just help me get home, kid."

Her father had called her *kid*, and John Braun knew that. How he'd recognized her through those wrecked eyes was a mystery to her.

"I'm calling. There's nothing you can say —"

His hand slipped into his corduroy jacket and produced a six-inch buck knife, stained red from tip to hilt.

"I plugged the bastards before they could do their

worst," he said. "If I end up in the E.R. with them, shit might get ugly."

She guided his hand back into his jacket and glanced at the sleepers. No one watched them, at least none that she could see. But somewhere there was a man with a six-inch hole in his gut, and he couldn't have gone far.

"All right, have it your way," she said, helping him to sit. "But if you don't tell me what the hell happened, I'm dumping you at the E.R. myself, understand?"

He'd been a friend of her father, and a regular at the bar since her family bought it in the late eighties. There wasn't a day she could remember that he wasn't seated at the far-left corner over a double vodka on the rocks with a lemon twist. You could order a *John Braun* and everyone knew what it was. And if you asked what he did for a living, he'd say he was in the retail business, or that he *sold things*. Any regular at a heavy-drinking dive knew it was code for *mind your fucking business.*

Now he was staggering half-dead under the fog-shot streetlamps of Pacific Avenue, keeping to the deepest shadows to avoid the eyes of graveyard shift cops. She kept him upright with one arm around his blood-slick waist, the other keeping his hand anchored to her shoulder.

"One more block," she said. "Can you make it?"

John Braun groaned in the affirmative.

She struggled to get him up the flight of stairs to his second story apartment. At number 203, a red eviction notice had been plastered over the door with bold black lettering. The brass door handle and deadbolt looked fresh from the package.

"Don't worry," he said in a wry whisper. "I know the locksmith. He owed me a favor."

He fumbled in his pocket for a shiny house key and she helped him do the unlocking. Inside, the apartment was dark and stale, but tidy. She thought she saw someone standing in the kitchen and the key dropped with a clatter. When the shape melted over the countertop and disappeared, she picked the key off the floor and helped the old man to the couch.

"You okay, kid?" said John Braun. He was plucking a pack of British cigarettes from a wooden box on the coffee table and tapping one out with blood-stained fingers. "You oughta take some time off. No offense, but you look terrible these days."

She laughed. "I guess that makes you a goddamn movie star."

"I'm ready for my close-up."

"You gonna tell me who's trying to kill you, or are you playing the edgy victim all night long? If I hurry, I can get four hours of terrible sleep before the waking nightmare starts all over again."

He winced when he smoked, whether it was the puckering or inhaling that hurt more, she couldn't tell. He coughed and shook his head.

"These are bad guys, kid. They don't like me one bit."

"I could have guessed both those things."

He reared an eyebrow and turned his hands up as if he knew he was stalling and wouldn't get away with it for long.

"Your father didn't want to saddle you with such a difficult business," he said, not looking at her when he said it, just squinting his wrecked eyes into the dark of the room. "We had something on the back burner, something that would help square up the bank loans and give you a little breathing room."

There was a bottle of Old Forester on the counter and she went to it and poured two glasses from the drying rack. She brought them to the coffee table and sat on the empty cushion beside John Braun without saying a word. She handed him a glass as if to say: *talk.*

"The first thing we had our eyes on didn't pan out," he said, struggling with the first sip of bourbon. He coughed and wiped his swollen mouth with his fingertips. "But it led to another thing, and right when we started working the angles, well, that's when your father —"

She knew her father had waged secret deals during the last year of his life as he grew more afraid of leaving her empty-handed. When his health declined, it made him even more desperate, almost conspiratorial. Now she was beginning to understand why.

"Go on," she said. "I know he wasn't perfect. Nobody is."

"Well, I got it done, kid. I found a way. I got my hands on the next thing we had our eyes on — but I didn't get away clean. Your father called it a cursed item — real Indiana Jones shit. And you know what? He was right. I'm convinced historians will draw a straight line from this one thing to the very downfall of human civilization. The object that brought us from the space age down to the stone age again, like hitting some kind of evolutionary iceberg."

"That's quite the buildup."

"Go to the microwave. Open it. There's a false back you can pull away."

She rose and went to the microwave and thumbed the rectangular door release. It was a cheap GE model with a clock display that flashed some sunnier hour than now. The door popped open and a tiny light flicked on.

"In the back?"

"Yeah, just reach in. There's a little string."

She found an inch-long piece of trussing twine in the corner and pulled the backing. It gave way and a dark passthrough appeared into the sheetrock behind it. The little light revealed a pinewood stud, electrical wiring, and a paper bag nestled in the insulation. She retrieved the bag and brought it back to the couch.

"You're telling me there's a cursed item in here?"

"Yeah, open it. See for yourself."

"It's not gonna — you know —" She danced her fingers in the air like a magic trick. *"Curse me?"*

He leaned back into the couch and smoked.

"The damage is done, kid," he said. "The whole world is cursed already."

She opened the bag and found a cube encased in bubble wrap. She pulled the bubble wrap away, revealing a shrink-wrapped white box with product information scrawled on the sides.

"Really, John? An iPhone?"

"Not just any iPhone. It's the first very first one from 2007. Four measly gigs. Sealed box. The last one sold at auction for two-hundred grand."

"Two-hundred grand?"

"Look it up. It's the real deal. Probably worth more by now."

She studied it for a moment before returning it to the bubble wrap with an amused grin. It was the kind of money that would go a long way in a tiny neighborhood bar.

"You have a buyer?" she asked.

"Sure do. There's a business card in the bag. A pawn-broker named Amos Friend up in San Francisco. If I can outrun the damn hellhounds, we may have ourselves a nice little payday, kid. It's the least I could do for what happened. Not to sound crazy, but I feel like your father's always hovering over me, making sure I hold up my end of the bargain. It's time for the ghosts to be at rest."

"I know the feeling."

She patted his leg and stretched, then handed him the brass door key.

He waved it off.

"Keep it," he said, rubbing his jaw tenderly. "Just in case."

John Braun wasn't at his anointed place at the bar the next day, and he didn't answer his phone when she called. She stopped by his apartment after closing and he didn't answer the door. She opened it and called for him, but the apartment was dark and quiet. He didn't respond the next day, either, and soon she was calling the hospitals and the local jail, looking for him.

Four days later, the police reported that the body of an elderly man had been found in the San Lorenzo River in an apparent homicide. Pooch Gilbert, another regular at the bar from the old days, had the inside scoop.

"My friend at the coroner says he has long gray hair," said Pooch over a Seven-and-Seven. Pooch had kind, slippery eyes, and a half-cocked smile typical of good-natured drunks. "No wallet, though. They're trying to identify him by his fingerprints. He said he'd been shot in the head like an execution. It's gotta be him. It's gotta be John Braun."

"You don't know that for sure," she said. But the empty spot in the corner hadn't been empty for decades, and now the void had begun to whisper as the morning dragged on:

come find me, kid. She wondered if it wasn't John Braun doing the whispering, but the cursed item in its lonely hidey-hole, waiting to be claimed. She opened the register and fished out two drink chips and slid them in Pooch's direction. "Can your friend get me an appointment to see the body?"

His half-smile became fuller and brighter.

"I'm a sucker for free booze," he said. "But so you know, if it's John Braun, they'll want to get a detailed statement from you. They'll want to know everything you know, so you should be prepared for that."

She flicked another drink chip his way.

"You're right — good thinking. Think you could cover the bar for an hour?"

His head swiveled left and right, regarding the two lonely drunks on either side of him.

"I can handle Bernie and Tom," he said. "But what do I do if a non-regular walks in? Some college kids or something?"

"Tell them we're closed for repairs."

He slipped off his stool and wandered behind the bar with his eyes twinkling as if he'd discovered some robber baron's vault. He picked up a rag and wiped at the stainless faucet.

"You know, I can probably do this for you all afternoon," he said.

"I bet you could."

"I mean it. Not for any pay or drink chips, either. Just so you can get some rest. We've been worried about you, you know. You're starting to look like your father before —"

She patted him on the shoulder. "Nice catch, Pooch."

"Just get some rest is all I'm saying. Go see about John Braun then get some goddamn sleep, why don't you? I'll even make Bernie mop the floors."

She put three gallons of gas in the sun-blistered Corolla and headed across town to the coroner's office. It was a drab setup with four or five cubicles and a small office for the lieutenant in charge of the unit. She waited only a minute or two before a young deputy named Dormer greeted her with a tentative handshake and an uneasy smile. He wore a fleece jacket with a yellow sheriff star, his name embroidered underneath.

"You said you haven't seen your uncle in a few days?" he asked. She'd told him all of this over the phone, but now he had a cautious attitude about it — maybe an instinct he was acting on.

"That's right," she said. "I see him almost every day, so it's unusual not to hear from him. I'm hoping for the best."

"But you haven't filed a missing persons report?"

"I intended to. But then I read the news —"

Dormer waved a hand to say *don't worry about it.*

"I understand," he said. "If you can help us with the ID, we'd appreciate it."

He brought her to a small room with a viewing window, like the kind she'd seen in the nursery unit at the local hospital. Only this window offered a much different scene. A door opened in the adjacent room, and Dormer appeared, rolling a gurney topped with a shrouded body. A brown stain mottled the sheet and she began to feel a nervousness in her legs. Dormer pushed a button on an intercom and told her he was going to remove the sheet and that the body had suffered a fair amount of trauma. She nodded and the deputy folded the sheet down to the bare chest.

"Is this your uncle, ma'am?" said Dormer.

She stood with her hand to her mouth, eyes full of tears.

John Braun lay with his hair still wet and stringy and fouled with grime. The left side of his face — the side farthest from the window — looked contused and very bloody. She supposed that if he'd been shot in the head, the bullet might have exited there and took his eye with it.

"Ma'am?"

She remembered the old days at the bar, her father shaking cocktails, John Braun telling jokes she wasn't old enough to understand. She remembered how the whole bar would laugh at his jokes, even if they weren't that funny. He just had a way of making it funny no matter what. She knew that even if they weren't that close, he was the closest connection she had to her father.

To anyone, really.

"Ma'am, is this your uncle?"

"No," she said, eyes spilling over. "Definitely not him."

She bolted out of the viewing room and down the hall and didn't stop until she'd crossed the parking lot and was sitting in the Corolla, weeping against the steering wheel. It was drizzling now, a blurry smear on the windshield. The day had turned dark.

She sent a message to Pooch: DONE HERE. MAKING ANOTHER QUICK STOP.

She started the car and cranked the fog vents to full blast.

Pooch wrote back: WAS IT HIM???

She started to answer, then thought better of it and deleted what she'd written.

She set a ten-minute timer on her phone and waited outside John Braun's apartment — watching the street and the stairwell. Looking for any sign of trouble. The bell rang at the junior high down the way. Teenagers came moping down the sidewalks, anchored to their screens like grim hunchbacks. The drizzle hadn't let up, and the windows of the Corolla had gradually succumbed to a wet fog. By the time the alarm went off, the neighborhood had become unknowable to her.

She fitted her knife ring over her knuckle and stepped to the street, toward the stairwell. A teenage boy nearly collided with her as he passed and she fumbled the brass key. She tisked and threw the boy a hot look, but he didn't seem to notice what had happened, just shuffled past with his hat pulled low. When she reached the door, she found it open. Inside, the apartment had been turned upside down. They'd flipped the couch, emptied the cupboards. Kitchen trash lay strewn over the carpet.

She went to the microwave. The door was open, light on.

She searched the false back for the string and found it, pulled it open. The bag lay where she'd last seen it, tucked neatly into the fiberglass insulation like the world's most impossible Easter egg, the bubble-wrapped box inside. She brushed the dust off and turned to the door. A man stood watching her in the doorway. He was young, with a shaved head and a crucifix tattoo over his right eyebrow. He didn't say a word, just hurried toward her with his hands reaching, that singular look of a man committed to his task. This time, she knew it wasn't a waking dream.

"Get the fuck away from me," she warned, but he'd already closed the distance, one hand driving her backwards, the other reaching for the box. He pinned her to the wall, trying to pry the thing out of her hand, saying *give it, give it, you bitch.* She'd been wearing the knife-ring for over two years and had never used it, but every time she slipped it on, a montage played in her mind — a jab to the eye, a flurry of quick stabs to the face. In some darker reveries, she'd tear at the carotid artery and release a geyser of gore like some 1980s horror flick. But it didn't happen that way, at least not quite. He'd nearly taken what he wanted when she struck him in the wrist, and before he pulled away, she punched him once in the face. He stumbled, blood pumping into his hand and curtaining down his face. She'd cut him in the space between his eyes, and the blood blinded him. He tried to wipe it away but he only managed to smear it deeper under the lids.

She shoved him hard. He teetered backward over the upturned coffee table and fell into a pile of rank kitchen trash. She fled out the door and was at the top of the landing when another man came running up the stairs. He flashed a knife with a fixed blade and slowed, one step at a time like a stalking cat.

"Give me the box, sweetheart," he said, with a silver-toothed grin. "No need to lose those pretty green eyes over it."

A shout came from the apartment. The first man was now staggering through the door with his blood-soaked shirt and gory face, blood dribbling from his radial artery onto the welcome mat. The second man had climbed another two steps and was very close now, but when he saw his partner, he slowed and pointed his knife with a horrified look.

"What the fuck happened to you?" he said.

She thought it would be the only advantage she'd get. She'd never kicked anyone in the face before, but one hard-heeled kick sent him clambering against the railing — enough for her to bolt down the stairwell, across the sidewalk, and into the street. When she reached the Corolla, she started digging for her car keys — but the car looked slumped and crooked on the chassis. Then she saw the knife slits in the sidewalls and the deflated lip of rubber flattening over the road.

Fuck.

She forged the center of the street as the two men shouted after her, their soles clapping on the wet asphalt. The drizzle had worsened to a steady rain, and she ran with sweat and rainwater stinging her eyes. She passed a covered bus stop — lonely figures bent mindlessly over the faint glows of their phones. They didn't look up as she stomped past. She clutched the bubble-wrapped box to her chest and tried to call 9-1-1 with her free hand, but she couldn't launch the call app without the men gaining on her.

She hooked right onto River Street and sprinted along the levee where tent cities had sprouted among the cattails, tattered nylon tents listing and sun-faded like some failed Boy Scout jamboree. The bloody man had fallen back, but the man with the knife hadn't quit the race. She kept to the levee, breath heavy in her chest, looking for a place to lose her tail. She thought she could see figures floating over the riverbank, beckoning her into the water with spectral arms. The levee brought her to the Broadway Street Bridge, and here, she finally ran out of breath.

The man wasn't far behind.

"Man, you can run," he said, as if the praise held any meaning. He stood hunched, hands on his knees, sucking air. By now it was rush hour, and cars were backing up on the bridge with their wipers on, drivers scrolling their social media feeds as they waited for the light to turn.

"You'll never take this from me," she said. She was trying the door handles on the cars stopped along the bridge, banging on the windows for help. She looked like a vagrant in the throes of a meth psychosis. Nobody looked up.

The man spat and coughed. Maybe it was a laugh.

"Looking for a ride, sweetheart? You know, I'm going to take that thing from you even if I have to cut it out of your hand."

She held the box between her knees and slipped one arm from her jacket. Then she fed the box into the tunnel of her empty sleeve and made a knot with the cuff. A heavy downpour swept over the bridge, wind howling through the concrete girders. The river had picked up. A churning white froth in the cattails below. She saw them again — spritely forms calling her name. They were telling her the current wasn't too strong.

"Don't you think about it," said the man. He'd nearly caught his breath and was inching closer now, his hand hidden in his jean jacket where the knife sat waiting to be drawn. "You'll ruin it. It'll be worthless."

"Maybe." She climbed atop the railing, wet hair flagging in the storm. The sky turned white and a thunderclap swept over the city. "But I'm taking the chance. I'm tired of working so fucking much. Or maybe I'm just tired. And maybe — maybe — John Braun had the box shrink-wrapped in heavy plastic so it wouldn't get wet no matter what."

The man glanced over the slick railing.

He took another step closer.

"Just come down from there," he said. He had no sway with her, but he tried anyway. He was just another downtown mope with a knife. "Get down. You'll die if you jump."

She looked out over the gray city, the drowning city. She wondered what it had looked like before they dumped asphalt over the wetlands. Before they clear-cut the redwoods and built up the levees. She wondered what a real river looked like without concrete edges. She could almost see it a century ago — no, three centuries. She could see the Ohlone in their tule boats and feathered capes, skimming the glassy waters with push poles. The shape of humankind had changed, she thought. Once straight-backed and proud, now caught in the sleazy glow of their devices, spines forming a grim question mark, asking *what are we now?*

John Braun had been right — the world was already cursed.

"Get out here, Dormer," said Sergeant Horvath, a grey-haired deputy with black whiskers in his ears. His rain slicker was dripping on the epoxy flooring. He pounded on the bathroom door with the ball of his fist. "You been in there twenty goddamn minutes. Hurry up and blow your wad."

A flush. The rattle of a belt buckle. The faucet hissed and went silent.

Dormer came out wiping his hands on his fleece jacket.

"What's the goddamn hurry?" he said.

"Miranda saw you with a woman yesterday. Late thirties with a gray streak in her hair."

"Yeah," said Dormer. He had the moon-eyed look of someone caught doing something inappropriate. "She came to ID the John Doe homicide vic."

"Did you get a name?"

"I have it written down at my desk. I was going to run it, but we got backed up and — why do you want to know?"

Horvath nodded to the morgue and Dormer followed. Miranda was standing over a body, still bagged and gurneyed. The lights flickered and brightened. Dormer could hear the generator kicking on. The woman's body had leaves in her hair, abrasions on the forehead. Hair sopping. It looked like she'd died in a flood.

"Christ," said Dormer. "Where'd you pick her up?"

"Some kids found her washed up on the jetty. Well?"

"Yeah," said Dormer. "Same woman. Any ID on her?"

"No. Just a phone in her pocket. Already gave it to forensics." Horvath went to the sink and fished out a black denim jacket. "She had this jacket half-on. You won't believe what we found tied up in the sleeve. It was all wrapped in bubble wrap."

Dormer took the box, still shrink-wrapped and pristine.

"An iPhone?"

"Not just any iPhone," said Horvath. "The first one ever made. Good luck watching PornHub on that thing."

Dormer stepped closer and tilted the woman's chin. The neck felt stiff, the body in full rigor. Most bodies had a stale and inanimate look, almost waxlike. But there was another expression at work here, like a hidden smile. A body enjoying the blissful nothingness of death.

The bone saw whined in the autopsy room.

Dormer stared into the image on the box.

"Anna," he said. "That was her name. Anna Reidy."

"What are the chances she was lying about knowing our John Doe?"

"Good chance, I'd say. Get a price on that iPhone and you'll know for sure."

"You know," said Horvath, "I remember when these things came out. Just before the Great Recession. I can't help but think that life was better back then, before everyone started gluing these goddamn things to their palms."

"It's the Golden Age fallacy," said Miranda, with her eyeglasses at the end of her nose like some wizened matriarch. She'd taken the box from Horvath and was turning it over in her hands. "It's an assertion based on an idealized conception of the past. Did you know that one of the oldest Sumerian clay tablets complains of the world going to shit? I guess it's always been bad, and it's always been getting worse. Bodies have been rolling through that door since my first day on the job and they're not stopping anytime soon. More and more every day. At least this one looks strangely restful."

They all looked at once and gave bland nods of agreement.

She did, in fact, look restful.

About the Author

CW Blackwell writes crime fiction set in the Central Coast of California. He is a two-time Derringer Award winner and four-time nominee. CW is a member of International Thriller Writers and the Short Mystery Fiction Society. His debut short story collection, *Whatever Kills the Pain*, will appear Summer 2025 from Rock and Hard Place Press. Find him on Bluesky: @cwblackwell.bsky.social.

HELLO, MARYLOU

SUSAN R. MORRITT

EMIL LEFEVRE IS his proper name, but his friends call him "Mimi." Not that Mimi *has* friends anymore. They're all dead and gone, just like most of his scattered family. But Mimi has his memories. Recollections of a beautiful girl with a shiny black ponytail, flawless pale skin, and the bluest eyes he's ever seen.

Mimi has come back to find Marylou. He knows she's here. Somewhere within the silence of the abandoned site where it all began. She's been here all along. Marylou.

Public Notice: An application has been proposed for a Land Change Zoning for this property.

The young man with the dark curls sweeping out in a wild arc from beneath his hard hat turned away from the sign he'd just posted to the steel gate. "I think we may have another problem. There's an old vagrant living in one of the buildings —" he began.

"Yes, I know," his companion interrupted. The older

man, dressed nattily in a suit and tie appeared out of place, despite the white hard hat. "We'll deal with *that* when the time comes."

Deal with that — and continue to pursue the planning process for the demolition of all the remaining barns and structures within the site of the now-defunct Lasalle Park Raceway. The massive hull of the grandstand still towered in the background, its rows of dirty windows staring out like bleary eyes across the neglected landscape. The image of an apocalyptic dream. Derelict barns, race office, blacksmith shops, cafeteria, dormitory, and paddock, in a once-orderly lineup alongside the weed-strewn racetrack. All awaiting the wrecking ball.

Only the bog, once enclosed by the training track at the rear of the property remained unchanged. The bog, an ecological bugaboo, standing in the way of a land developer's ambitious plans.

"Well, hello Marylou!" Webby Moore, coffee in hand, leaned against the door frame, and watched as the girl unhooked the sweaty horse from a jog cart.

Observing this scene, Mimi Lefevre scowled at his boss's words. This tired, often-repeated reference to an old song (long before Mimi's time) always irritated and embarrassed him, especially when it was directed towards *this* girl. Marylou — the most beautiful girl Mimi had ever laid eyes upon.

Marylou led her horse past the smiling Webby and paused as Mimi unsnapped the crosstie from his horse's halter to allow her to walk unimpeded down the shed row to her own stable of employment.

Mimi's eyes followed the girl, her tight blue jeans emphasizing the curve of her ample buttocks.

"Get a move on it, Mimi. I need to get this last trip in before qualifiers start," Webby admonished as he placed his coffee cup on the nearby tack box and turned away to fasten the chin strap on his helmet.

Mimi tore his gaze away from Marylou and reached for the bridle hanging from a harness bracket.

As Webby buckled the lines to the bit, he leaned over his much-shorter groom to whisper in Mimi's ear, "You're aiming pretty high there, son. She's out of your league —"

Mimi shot a withering glance towards his boss. *What the hell did the old bugger know, anyway?* Marylou. His goddess. His dream.

Max Gillies reminded Mimi of a gun fighter from an old black-and-white Western movie. Light on his feet for a squarely built, heavy-set middle-aged man, he walked with his arms slightly akimbo from his barrel-chested torso. *So-o-o* unlike his tall and lanky long-drink-of-water offspring. Where Max was swarthy — dark ferret eyes and black hair just beginning to turn grey, Carl was fair with butter-blond locks, and a golden-boy tanned face.

The golden boy. Pretty boy. Oh, how Mimi detested Carlton Gillies from the neighbouring stable. Burned with jealous resentment each and every day as he watched his "rival" cozy up to Marylou. Born with a silver spoon in his mouth. Even Webby said as much. It wasn't fair. At least from the perspective of the grubby little ragged Mimi Lefevre, a lowly groom with no advantages to his name.

The spring of 1980 arrived on the backstretch of Lasalle Park like a sweet sunshine burst of promise for the summer ahead with temperatures soaring unseasonably high. The young ladies residing in the women's dormitory built over one of the backstretch barns had commenced crawling out of their dorm room windows on hot afternoons to sunbathe on the roof.

Mimi, who lived in a mean little tack room off his stable's shed row, had heard about this phenomenon from his buddies. Cafeteria gossip, racetrack gossip passed between male grooms and trainers while jogging horses side-by-side. Heard about it, but Mimi had not witnessed this sight as of yet, but that was about to change. Oh, yes, because Marylou, *his* Marylou, lived in the women's dorm.

Mimi, freshly showered, and dressed in clean clothes strolled along in front of Barn H. Strolled... or strutted. It was debateable. With his heart in his mouth and a worried furrow above his hazel eyes, Mimi paused and gazed upwards to hopefully catch a glimpse of his beloved. Low and behold, stretched upon the full length of a reclining lawn chair, was the girl of his dreams. Long, shapely legs, pale against the bright canary yellow webbing of her throne. Marylou, Queen of Lasalle Park Raceway backstretch.

"Marylou. Hey, Marylou," Mimi shouted. "Catchin' a few rays?"

Marylou leaned forward in the chair, her black ponytail swinging. "Hi Mimi." She waved at the figure below who stood transfixed, gazing up worshipfully.

Mimi heard a titter of laughter from Marylou's companions on the roof and looked away, his face flushing. Turning around, he started towards the cafeteria. "See you later,

Marylou." His words, flung over his shoulder elicited another round of giggles from the rooftop.

So be it. The image of those long bare legs which seemed to stretch to infinity from her cut-off blue jeans shorts was worth the derisive sound of the other girls' laughter. *Perfection. Thy name be Marylou.*

The meet at Lasalle Park was drawing to a close. The highlight of the final scheduled card included the Walkers Cup for the top Free-for-All pacers from Canada and across the nearby U.S. border.

Webby Moore's stable was racing their Invitation trotter, Camp Cookie, for a hefty purse on this final day of the race meet. The Gillies Stable, however, were truly in the limelight for the afternoon, with a horse entered to race in the Cup, although the odds cast him as a long shot.

Mimi, cleaning harness, felt his eyes straying to Marylou as she brushed down their stable's entry. Red River Byrd, the shining star of Max Gillies' barn, was a handsome four-year-old chestnut stallion with a wavy foretop and mane. Sixteen-two hands high, "Red" was a muscular powder keg of energy, prone to bouts of temper with any male handler, but most often a pussycat for his regular groom, Marylou.

"Think Red's worth a bet?" Mimi called down the shed row.

Marylou paused and momentarily turned away from Red. "Maybe. He's sharp today. Dragging me around when I was —" Her words were cut short as a roar erupted from the stallion, who then proceeded to jump sideways, trampling upon Marylou's running-shoe clad foot.

"*You* did that!"

Mimi's head snapped around as his boss stormed past him and the stricken Marylou, who had managed to hobble over to a trunk to sit down.

"What kind of a stupid stunt was that?"

Carl began backing away, but not quick enough before Webby reached out to toss him against a stall door.

"Dunno what you're talking about," Carl mumbled, turning his perfectly coiffed blonde head away.

Webby, his face still a thundercloud, stared at the young man. "Pinching his neck and jumping back. *Teasing him* —"

Mimi, now firmly entrenched at Marylou's side, watched as Webby shook his head with disgust before turning away to return to his own stable.

"That punk should have his ass kicked."

Mimi could not have agreed more.

"The starter has called for the horses. It's post time for the ninth race."

Mimi glanced back one more time at the undersized mare in the crossties. Boots and bandages on, bridled, with lines buckled to the bit. All he had to do was hook her to the bike. He had just enough time to run out and watch the big race. Through the open door, he spied Marylou squeezed in with the crowd against the fence.

"The field of nine pacers for the Walker's Cup are behind the starting gate. And they're off and pacing —"

As the horses swept by heading to the half-mile marker, Mimi watched as Gene Caldwell, the Gillies Stable's driver of choice, pulled Red to flush cover second over.

"Three quarters in 1:27 flat."

"Come on, Red! Come on, Red!" Marylou shouted, excitedly.

Three wide, four wide around the last turn, and down the stretch. "They're at the wire, and it's too close to call."

Mimi turned to Marylou and touched her arm. "I think Red got there."

The lovely Marylou beamed at Mimi, then picked up her cooler-blanket and pail before limping to the track entrance.

As Mimi dashed back into the building, he almost collided with his boss, who was heading in the same direction. They only had five minutes until post parade to have Camp Cookie hooked and tied down to the sulky. Maybe this would prove to be an all-around lucky afternoon for their shed row of Barn D, Lasalle Park Raceway. Fingers crossed.

Let the celebration begin...

The aroma from barbeques drifting between barns. Sizzling hamburgers, sausages, hot dogs, steaks.

Grooms walking blowing horses, their nostrils still flaring with exertion. Fly sheets or simply towels draped over their kidneys as they were watered out, cooled out. Displayed with pride like the newly reigned king and queen of Lasalle Park — Red River Byrd, the winner of the Walkers Cup, and the diminutive Camp Cookie, who had proven she could take on the boys.

Webby Moore — grass roots trainer/driver from the Ottawa Valley, Ontario, Canada. Holding his nose long enough to share a celebratory drink with his neighbour —

Max Gillies, trainer/big-shot wheeler dealer agent from Dayton, Ohio, U.S.A.

His overweening son, Carlton Gillies, scrubbed and spotless in his white collared polo shirt and starched designer shorts. Fresh from the grandstand lounge.

Marylou Stevenson, of backwater, nowhere Michigan, U.S.A, limping up and down the shed row as she fed and watered the horses, then swept the floor before finally joining in the festivities.

Farriers, owners, track maintenance workers and cafeteria staff, letting loose, with case after case of Old Vienna Lager and Molson Golden Ale. Bottle after drained bottle, after drained bottle...

And Mimi Lefevre, of Drummondville, Province of Quebec, Canada. Downing whatever brew was put in his hand, be it in a Styrofoam cup or half-full flask. Tying the loop, loop-dee-loop in ever-tighter knots. Until a freebie of Mister Bill's blotter acid sent him on a trip which rendered the grubby little groom stretched out in a stupor alongside the boggy pond at the edge of the back training track. Amid the dragon flies and horse flies. Under the blue sky, which threatened to be obscured by dark clouds rolling in from the west. Rolling in to the chorus of bull frogs and distant thunder.

"Oh-h-h... Ta-bar-nak." A sigh, muted groan. A whispered oath, as Mimi struggled to rejoin the living. His eyelids flickered open, shut, open. Blinking. His face contorted as the sheets of rain, sweeping like a gigantic opaque broom, pelted his bare arms. Streaming rivulets from his plastered hair over his eyebrows, down his chin, dripping down his neck.

There it was. Again. The noise. Crying. A wail. Louder... Primordial sounds evolving into syllables. A female voice. Marylou's voice. *Get off me. No. No. No-o-o...*

Time ticking. With a supreme effort, Mimi raised himself up onto his elbow and peered through the darkness, the rain. For a split-second, the downpour paused, as if gulping an intake of breath, and Mimi made out the figure of someone running with a pronounced limp across the sodden ground.

Oh God. Help me. Carl. Carl —

Mimi felt a tremendous blow to his back. It knocked him forward into a crumpled ball, causing him to fall sideways until his head struck the ground with a dull thud. A foot nudging him... then, mercifully, oblivion once again descended, freeing ragged little Mimi, the lowly groom, from the horror, panic he'd felt arise with the realization of what he thought he'd just witnessed.

The young man with the dark curly hair set down his coffee cup to don his hard hat. He needed a haircut. He hated how his hair swept up like wings around his face. As he glanced out the door of the trailer, he cursed his boss. The fog was thick as pea soup, yet there it was on his cell phone — the message ordering him to begin clearing the brush from around the bog.

He'd read the letter from the ministry. *Until further notice, there is to be no felling of trees or brush on the site of the former Lasalle Park Raceway.* How convenient, how ingenious of his boss to decide to defy the order and clear the land on a day when the public could not possibly witness it... and what a headache for himself to even attempt it. Even with the headlights on the tractor, he'd be working close to blind. Maybe he should ask for a raise.

Mimi Lefevre turned away from the back door of Pompeii's Pizzeria. He knew the smoke break hours of every eatery in the neighbourhood and the free pizza slices were still warm in his pockets. Snug and dry, wrapped inside the over-sized industrial rain slicker, the misty fog did not bother him. Back in the early spring, a construction worker had taken pity on him on a particularly brutal morning of cold sleet. "Hey old-timer, wait here and I'll help you out." The young fellow had disappeared into the company trailer to return with a brand-new raincoat as a gift. "It will never be missed," he assured Mimi, with a friendly pat on the shoulder.

The lump, however, which had recently appeared under his jaw, *did* in fact bother Mimi. Oftentimes he was dizzy and momentarily unsteady on his feet. No worries. Clad in his "tent," he had no qualms of a picnic in the fog, cushioned by the long grass. Now, as he cut through the gap in the fence which enclosed the site of the former racetrack, Mimi was content. A full bottle of seven-dollar Reisling wine nestled like a demanding lover within his filthy coveralls. Despite the fog, which lay like a ghostly entryway to another world, Mimi was sure every step he took drew him nearer to the bog. The bog... and Marylou.

Where was Marylou? The shipping van had arrived to transport the horses across the border to the racetrack in Ohio where the Gillies Stable would race until Lasalle Park re-opened. Max Gillies had loaded his pickup truck with race bikes and harness bags... *but where was Marylou?*

Carl had insisted he'd last seen her the evening before, heading through the stable gate with a strange young man unknown to himself. Someone who'd shipped in?

Mimi, hung over and barely functioning, had locked his bleary eyes with Carl's evasive pale peepers to no avail. The golden boy was sticking to his story.

And so, the years passed. For the first ten years or so, Mimi recalled seeing a sign posted in race offices across the country. *Have you seen this girl?* A picture of his beloved.

Torn down from the bulletin board of a B track where he'd briefly worked, Mimi still carried the notice. Close to his heart.

The fog was finally beginning to show signs of dissipating with the occasional ray of fleeting sunshine. The young man with the hard hat and dark curly hair swung the tractor and roaring brush hog machine around. One more turn and he would call it quits. Just as the sun broke through to illuminate the landscape, he pulled the key from the ignition and stepped out of the cab to a scene straight from hell. Bloody bits of scarlet-hued confetti littered the razed ground and banners of dripping human flesh hung from surrounding untouched shrubbery.

Retching. Doubled over disbelief and denial in the face of what a brief few minutes before was simply a job order well executed.

Emil Lefevre is his proper name, but his friends call him "Mimi." With his friends and most of his family dead and gone, Mimi has come back to find Marylou — the girl with the black ponytail, flawless pale skin, and the bluest eyes he's ever seen. Marylou, his dream, his goddess. He will wrap his loving arms around her to keep her safe and warm. She's been here all along. Marylou.

About the Author

Susan R. Morritt is a writer, visual artist, and musician from Waterford, Ontario, Canada. Her work has appeared in numerous journals and anthologies including *34 Orchard Journal, Cosmic Horror Monthly, Does It Have Pockets, Third Estate Art Decapitate Journal,* and is upcoming in *Inflated Graveworm,* and *Rough Diamonds.* She was short-listed for The Staunch Short Fiction Prize, long-listed for The Redbud Writing Project Coppice Prize, as well as others. Susan is a former racehorse trainer who earned her Diploma in Creative Writing and Fundamentals of Journalism while working full time with livestock.

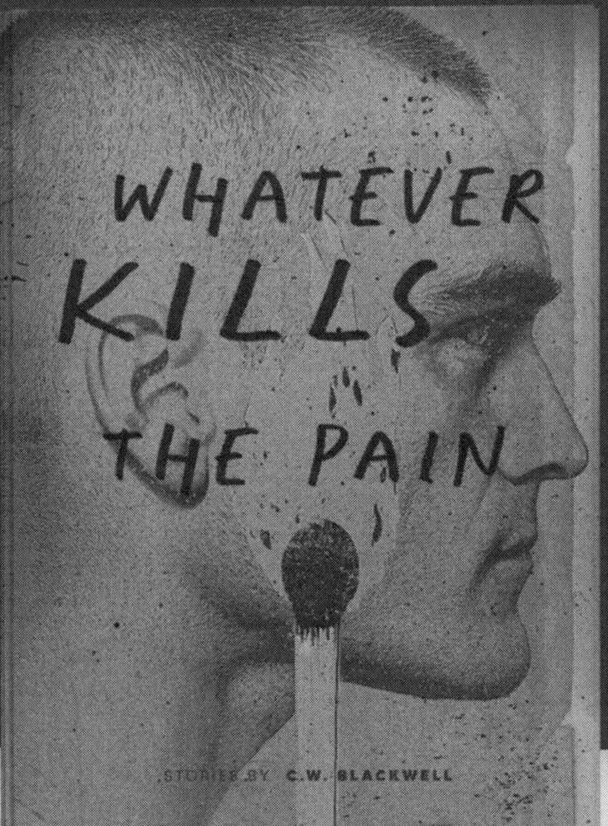

WHATEVER
KILLS
THE PAIN
STORIES BY C.W. BLACKWELL

Made in the USA
Columbia, SC
30 May 2025

58680209R00102